Words are like Birds

Words are like Birds

Eryl Samuel

Contents

Waiting for Lift-off

IGNITION

At first, there is nothing. Only empty space. A void without light.

Then, from nowhere, a quivering fragment of life bleeps in the nothingness, like the pings from a black-box. In the mists of time before time, the ping becomes a pulse, becomes a beat, and you are thrust from the darkness into a choking ocean of air and wailing light. You blink and screech angrily at the world, clinging to the warmth of your mother's breast.

An unshaven face appears above you, infusing your newly formed lungs with tobacco smoke and cheap cologne. 'My God it's ugly,' says the face. 'Is it a girl or a boy or what?'

'He's a boy, look!'

'Wow, a chip off the old block, I'd say.'

Your father grins. For a few seconds he looks deep into your eyes, as if searching for something. Then he shakes his head and laughs.

'Bloody hell, Meg, we made this thing together. You and me. I can't fucking believe it!'

You are indeed a miracle. You are unique. You are the most precious thing in the whole of the cosmos. There are no limits to where you will go or what you will become.

You are Sam.

ONE

The photograph is on the mantelpiece in the front room, but few people see it. Other than for Sunday lunch, the room is rarely used. It's only opened for the most important guests, such as the Vicar or your Aunty Gwen. When they visit, you are marched in for inspection. They pat you on the head and say, 'My, hasn't he grown.'

Then they say, 'I hear you're taking piano lessons, Sam, won't you play us something?'

You shake your head, but Mum opens the piano and plonks you on the stool. You sit staring at the blurred black and white keys.

'Don't be shy, play them *Three Blind Mice.*'

Your hands are clammy and your mind is blank. You can't remember where to start. You can't remember anything. You turn and bury your head in your mother's lap to hide your blushing and your tears.

'Never mind, some other time,' they say. You catch them glancing pityingly at your mother.

After they have gone, you sneak back into the room and pull down the faded photograph from the mantelpiece and stare at it in wonder. In it, a little curly-haired boy is waddling across the floor in a nappy. He seems happy, dangling his hands in the air, like a puppet without strings. As if he is floating.

On the back of the photograph it says: *Sam's first steps.*

But you don't recognise him. You cannot make the connection.

TWO

This is your first memory. You are sitting in the old pram in the yard sailing across a big ocean, bellowing at the fishes that glisten in the water all around you. Mum is in the kitchen, listening to the radio.

The next moment she is in the yard, in the middle of your sea, stepping on dolphins. There are tears in her eyes.

'Are you alright, Mummy?'

She cradles you in her arms. She says, *I love you, sweetheart,* over and over through her sniffles. On the radio there is something about a mountain falling on a school, somewhere far away.

Later, you hear Daddy come home and you creep down the stairs. There is a spade propped against the wall by the door and Mummy is cuddling Daddy in her arms, the same way she held you earlier. Daddy's face is dirty and black except for two thin white lines winding down his cheeks.

He looks like a sad clown.

THREE

The birds scatter on the path as you stomp among them on your little bandy legs, giggling and shouting. You are cosy, wrapped up in a bobble hat and mittens.

'Look, Mummy!'

You throw the bread from the bag into the air so that the crumbs fall over your head like confetti. The ducks and geese squawk and flap their wings excitedly. But Mummy isn't watching. She's puffing on her cigarette, eyes shut.

'Shall we go to the park and play?' she says.

The park will be full of silly children, mimicking your running with their in-turned feet and floppy hands. Mummy will be too busy smoking and talking with the other mothers to notice. The doctor at the infirmary says you will grow out of it. That you just need to strengthen your muscles. If you practise walking like a penguin and balancing on one leg like a flamingo, you will get better.

'I don't like the see-saw or the woundabout,' you say, 'they make me sick.' You clamber back into the pushchair. 'I want to go home.'

FOUR

You are sitting on Dad's lap driving when he suddenly yanks the steering wheel and rams into the side of Mum's car. Mum shrieks.

'We got her good, boyo,' says Dad.

Mum turns around and glares.

'Ooh, was that you, Sam Bennett?' she shouts. 'I'm going to get you for that.'

Mum sounds cross, but you know she's only joking. You shout back:

'We got you, Mum!'

Mum spins her dodgem round and accelerates straight towards you. Dad thrusts down on the pedal and speeds towards Mum. You close your eyes and scream as the bumpers collide with a jolt. When you look up, Mum and Dad are laughing, so you squeal and kick with laughter too.

Afterwards, Dad buys you a candy floss. It's like a pink sugary cloud. You try snapping at its fluffy edges with your teeth, but it sticks to your mouth and nose. There are stalls and music and lights and people everywhere, even though it's dark now. When you are older and think of happy times, you will remember this moment.

On the way back to the caravan, Mum stops and gazes up at the moon.

'It's amazing to think that last week there were people up there, walking on its surface,' she says. 'Yet the furthest I get to go, is bloody Trecco Bay!'

This is something else you will always remember.

FIVE

'Is God watching us now?'

You are on the way home from church. You're holding a picture you coloured in with crayons in Sunday school. It shows Jesus feeding the five thousand with fish and chips.

'Yes, God is always watching us, making sure we're safe.'

'Is he even watching when I have a wee?'

'I think he looks away when you're having a wee. He's not very interested in little boys weeing.' Mum is smiling.

'What about Dad, because Dad never goes to church?'

'No he doesn't, does he?'

'When is Dad coming home, Mummy?'

'I don't know, darling. Soon, probably.' Mummy says this without looking at you. You have to wait while she pulls a tissue from her sleeve, and fumbles in her handbag for her sunglasses. The ones that make her look like a spy. She clutches your hand tightly and you walk home together in silence, your feet click-clacking on the pavement.

SIX

You kick the ball and it trickles between the mole-hills under Dad's despairing dive.

'Great goal, Jairzinho!'

Jairzinho plays for Brazil. You know this because you have a sticker of him in your Mexico World Cup album. Dad says he's really good, even better than John Toshack.

'When are you going to take me to the football, Dad?'

'Next season, Sam, I promise.'

Dad kicks the ball back to you, but you're more interested in the rocket behind him. You've never seen it up close before. It looks like the frame of Thunderbird 1, pointing up to the sky. Mum says that there's a top secret space station hidden under the mountain with a launch pad, just like on Tracy Island. Only very important people know about it.

When you tell Dad this, he chuckles. 'That's typical of your mother. What other nonsense has she been spouting?'

'She said you'd been abducted by an alien.'

Dad picks up the football and wrinkles his face. 'Abducted by an alien?'

'Yes, an alien with a short skirt and long blonde hair. She said it had turned your brain to mush.'

SEVEN

'One, two, three, four, five, six, seven.' You gleefully count the spaces as you move Mum's Top Hat along the board. 'Welcome to Vine Street and my lovely hotel,' you say, rubbing your hands together. 'That will be £400, please.'

Mum looks glumly at her funds.

'I think you've won,' she says, handing over all the notes she's got. There's well over six hundred pounds there, but Mum says she needs to finish. She wants to make tea before Morecambe and Wise.

Mum disappears into the kitchen with a glass of sherry and a cigarette, so you pack the game away and go upstairs. You like winning, but it's not much fun when she doesn't try. Monopoly is never much fun with just the two of you. You sit on the bed and read your Beano annual. Again.

When Dad calls around the next day, he's wearing a blue and white scarf.

'Happy Christmas, big boy. You didn't think your dad had forgotten you, did you?' He picks you up and swings you round and round. His moustache tickles when he kisses you.

You unwrap the parcel while he waits in the hall. It's the Beano annual and a large Dinky truck. 'Thank you,' you say shyly. You don't really like Dinky trucks. They're the wrong size. Dad has forgotten that you collect Matchbox cars.

Mum doesn't say much. She is staring over Dad's shoulder at the Cortina parked outside. There's a woman sitting there. She has long blonde hair.

After a few minutes, the horn beeps.

'I better be off,' says Dad. 'I gotta get down the footie. I'll give the City a shout for you, eh Sam?'

As Dad drives away, you can hear Mum lighting another cigarette behind you.

EIGHT

It's a Friday night, so there is no school tomorrow. You're lying on your bed reading *The Island of Adventure*. Smokey is curled up at your feet, purring.

When Mum calls for you to come downstairs, you hope she's made you a Horlicks. But Mum is sitting in the living room next to Uncle Simon. There are two wine glasses on the coffee table in front of them. Uncle Simon is quite funny and nice, but he stinks of perfume and he doesn't know much about football.

'We need to tell you something, Sam,' says Mum. Her voice is croaky. 'I want you to know that I love you more than anything in the world, darling.'

You roll your eyes. Mum always gets a bit soppy and silly when she's been drinking.

'And Uncle Simon, he loves you too, don't you, Simon?'

Uncle Simon is fidgeting with your toy soldiers. He mumbles and nods. His face is flushed. You yawn. You wish Mum would get to the point, you want to go back to your book.

'Well, Sam, it's just that Mummy and Simon have become very fond of each other too, and...' Mum clears her throat. 'Well, we've decided we need a bit of time together. Alone.'

Simon is examining a Stormtrooper in his palm. Mum looks as if she's going to cry. If they want to be alone, you wonder why they've called you down to the room.

'So, we're going away for a while. To travel, while we're still young.'

You are confused. 'For how long?'

'I'm not sure. A few months. Maybe a year. I've arranged for you to stay with your father and Christine. Until we're settled.'

'Does that mean I won't be living here?'

'No, darling, you won't. None of us will be living here.'

You can't process what Mum has just said. All you can think about is the cat.

'What about Smokey, where will she live?'

Mum purses her lips, but doesn't answer.

NINE

'Cat got your tongue, boy? What's wrong with you?'

You glare up at the headmaster, your fists still clenched.

'He started it. He was calling me names and saying things about my mother.' You can feel your eyes twitching, but you're determined not to cry.

'Mrs Williams saw you hit him first, and there's no excuse for that, whatever he might have said. Sticks and stones, boy, sticks and stones.'

The headmaster jabs his stubby finger against your forehead.

'You really need to curb that temper of yours. This is the second time in a fortnight. I don't know what it was like in your old school, but we will not tolerate behaviour like that here. Do you understand?'

You stare up at him mutely.

'Do. You. Understand?' Mister Jenkins stands over you and swishes the cane through the air.

'Yes.'

'Yes, what?'

'Yes, Sir.' Your voice is no more than a faint squeak now.

'Good. I'm sure your parents didn't bring you up to behave like a little hooligan. I don't enjoy doing this, but you need to be taught a lesson. Bend over the desk, Sam!'

Slowly, you bend over and close your eyes.

Beam me up, Scotty, you think. *Please, beam me up and take me away from here. Anywhere will do.*

TEN

The city is spread out in front of you like a magic carpet, an intricate pattern of houses, roads and offices. It's hard to believe that a quarter of a million people are living down there. You try to locate your old house. You remember Mum saying it was in one of the terraced rows with the red-tiled roofs.

Dad and Christine are behind you on the rug with little Natalie. She is toddling around on reigns, gurgling and giggling. You may as well be invisible.

Thunderbird 1 still looms above the trees behind them. Dad says it's just a telecommunications tower. It looks to you like a dinosaur skeleton now, left over from when space rockets ruled the Earth. Anyway, you've stopped pretending to be Scott or Virgil Tracy. You know there is no International Rescue to save you, no pretty lady in a pink Rolls-Royce to whisk you away. The fact is, you look more like Brains. A gormless Brains in NHS glasses and a knitted jumper. A Special Needs Brains.

You haven't had a postcard or letter from Mum for ages now. You wonder if she's down there in the city somewhere. Maybe she's back in the old house, singing and smoking in the kitchen. Perhaps your old bedroom is just as it was: the soldiers and Matchbox cars you left behind, scattered on the floor. The Spitfires and Messerschmitts hanging from the ceiling. The sticker albums and annuals and Enid Blyton books. The Scalextrix and Shoot football-league tables and tabs. The jars of marbles. The seashells from Porthcawl.

But those days are gone. You're old enough to know that you can't go back to how it was. Time crawls forwards, not backwards. Slowly. Imperceptibly. You have no option but to wait as each day morphs gradually into night; as the days become weeks and the weeks become months and the months become years.

In three years' time, the Sex Pistols will play the Castle Cinema over the mountain in Caerphilly and your teenage self will pick up a guitar and start thrashing furiously at some chords. A new Sam will be born and your life will lift off. Properly, this time.

But you don't know that yet. For now, there is no punk. There is no future. There's only nothingness. Emptiness. Days stretching out into eternity like milky-ways.

All you can do is wait. For something to happen. For something to change.

The Birthday Gift

At first I stand transfixed – mesmerised by the deep crevice of cleavage and the outline of her breasts beneath her shirt. They protrude tantalisingly like full ripe fruit draped under a thin cloth on a hot summer's day. I'm almost salivating. Is it wrong to feel like this about your own daughter?

My daughter. My beautiful daughter. She appeared on my doorstep fifteen minutes ago and now everything has changed. Her name is Rebecca, but she tells me her friends call her Becky. I don't know if I should call her Rebecca or Becky.

The truth is, I know very little about her. What I do know, or can surmise, is she's about twenty years old, she has long blonde hair, dark, strangely familiar eyes, looks damn good in tight-fitting jeans and... well,... she has great breasts! That's about it. This isn't much to know about your own daughter, I must concede, but twenty minutes ago, I didn't even know I had a daughter.

This was supposed to be a romantic night in for Lisa's birthday. Our first night alone in five years, since the birth of our son. Lisa has taken him over to her mothers' house. She'll be returning soon for the special celebration I'd promised her.

Then the doorbell rang. My initial grumpiness at the interruption to the feast I was preparing subsided when I saw this attractive young woman staring back at me. An attractive young woman with great breasts. I assumed that she'd come to collect some tupperware catalogue or charity envelope, but I felt an undeniable swelling of pleasure when she just looked at me and smiled. She seemed vaguely familiar, but I couldn't place her, so I smiled back. I wondered if Lisa had booked a child minder by mistake.

'Yes?' I inquire pleasantly

'Hello, Dad,' she says.

I hesitate, unsure of how to respond. Is this girl making some joke about my age at my expense? But then something clicks and I remember where I've heard that voice before, where I've seen her face. Even after all this time, I know who she is. She is the spit of her mother.

For a moment I stand frozen, in a confusion between fear and lust.

'You look as if you've seen a ghost,' she says in an accent I haven't heard for so many years. I stare at her, unable to speak or move.

'Hmm, something smells good. Were you expecting me?' she says brightly.

'It's my wife's birthday. She's dropping off my son at her mother's. She'll be back soon.'

I calculate that she should be back any minute now. I'm anxious. Now would not be a good time for my wife to find out that she may have a step-daughter. Today would be a very bad day for her to find this out.

'Oh, it's Lisa's birthday, is it? I'm sorry, but I haven't brought her a present.'

How does she know my wife's name? What's happening? I'm disorientated.

'May I come in?' she says. She seems calm and self-assured. Too self-assured for a girl meeting her father for the first time.

'Yes, I suppose you'd better come in,' I say, in the absence of any clear alternative strategy. 'Please excuse the mess.'

Rebecca, or should I say Becky, follows me into the living room. We step over the detritus of Morgan's discarded toys.

'I'm sorry, they're my son's,' I explain stupidly.

'Ah yes, Morgan. He's my brother, isn't he?' She scrutinises the boxes of lego and duplo, the random pieces of train set, the half-coloured drawings and games and books and DVDs strewn all over the carpet and shelves. The evidence is everywhere. The evidence of indulgence and excessive expenditure on a loved child.

Her brother? Hold on a moment, things are moving a bit too quickly. I wonder if this is some bizarre practical joke. I scan the room for a hidden camera. How do I know she is who she says she is? It seems churlish to ask your daughter for proof of identity, but I can't just take her word for it, can I?

'Morgan's my son. As far as I know, he's my only child,' I say.

'Oh, I see,' she says, 'you don't think I'm your daughter, do you? Perhaps you've forgotten? So many years of ignoring my existence. Let me jog your memory.'

She pulls something out from a torn brown envelope in her handbag and hands it to me. It's an old faded Polaroid. I see a picture of myself as a young man with long straggling hair sitting in a rowing boat. I recognise myself, but I don't recall the location or the photograph ever being taken. I think desperately. I know who her mother is. I know we made love. We were young and reckless and... carefree. But there was no child. At least, not when I left.

'Turn it over,' she says.

I turn the picture over. On the back in faded blue biro is written, 'Gareth (Becky's dad), Trentham Park, May 1996.'

I stare back into the mists of the past, trying to excavate some clear memory of the time and place. I find only a vague recollection of the day shipwrecked in a dark corner of my mind. But I remember her mother. I remember Kate. I remember a squalid damp downstairs flat in a brick terrace on Charlotte Street. I remember nights of clumsy, sweaty, drunken passion on her squeaky single bed. I remember a futile fling with a pretty local girl in the last months of University. I remember Kate alright. She was my beautiful distraction.

'Mum said you just up and left. After you graduated, you packed up and went back to Wales. She didn't know your address or have the slightest idea where in Wales you lived. She said she didn't even know your surname. You were just Gareth to her from Aber or Pont or Llan something, with a common surname like Evans or Jones or Davies or Williams. All she knew was that one day you were there and the next you'd gone. Disappeared for good. Only you left something important behind. You left me.'

I can feel my body quaking. This couldn't be true, could it?

'Are you sure?'

'Well I wasn't there, was I? But mum was sure. There was no one else. My birthday is January 26th 1997. Work it out for yourself.'

But I don't need to work it out. I know now where I've seen those eyes before. I've seen them thousands of times. I see them every time I look at my reflection in the mirror. I look at her and I know it's true.

I feel disgust. Disgust with my former self. Disgust with my current self that can so casually lust for a stranger who is my daughter. On my wife's birthday.

'How did you find me?' I ask.

'Facebook. I searched and eventually I found you. The right name, the right age, the right university, the right subject, the right picture.' She nods towards the photograph in my hand.

'I've changed,' I say, rubbing my thinning hairline.

'Have you?' she says.

I don't know what to say. I'm in a daze. In my mind the question arises. Why is she here? Why now? What does she want? But these questions seem too blunt.

'So, what would you like to do?'

She studies me carefully. I feel as if I am being examined. Assessed.

'I can't stay long,' she says. 'But wait a moment, Kate's in the car, she's dying to meet you, let me fetch her.' Becky stands and makes for the door.

My heart is pounding. I feel dizzy. Hundreds of questions are spinning in my head. My God, Kate is with her. What do I say to her? After all these years.

When Becky returns, Kate isn't with her. Instead, there's a little girl holding her hand. She's like a mini version of Becky, except she has a pony tail and freckles and has rounder, fuller cheeks. She's wearing a pink anorak and carrying a little doll.

'This is my daughter, Kate,' says Becky. 'I named her after my mother. Of course, you remember my mother, don't you?' Turning to the child she says, 'this man is your grandfather, he's been looking forward to meeting you, haven't you, Grandad?'

Neither of us say anything.

'Haven't you, Grandad?'

I look at little Kate. Little innocent Kate so lost and bewildered in this strange big peoples' world.

'Yes, Kate, of course I have, it's just a bit of a shock – I wasn't expecting you. Would you like a biscuit and a drink?'

'Yes please,' replies Kate timidly. 'Can I have a coke?'

'I'm afraid I haven't got any coke in at the moment. Let me see, we've got apple juice, is that okay?'

'Or champagne?' says her mother, indicating the bottle of bubbly and the empty wine glasses on the table behind.

Kate stands with her thumb between her teeth, rocking back and forth.

'Apple juice is just fine,' says her mother. 'Too much coke isn't good for you, Kate. I'm sure Grampy will give you much healthier food than Mummy does. He'll give you all good stuff to help you grow up to be big and strong and beautiful.'

My stomach lurches. Before I can say anything, Becky is speaking again.

'Kate was very upset when Grandma died. Well, we both were. Grandma, love her, hadn't been well for a long time. Even when Mummy was a little girl, Grandma was often unwell. She used to drink stuff that made her sick and a bit crazy. Mummy used to think sometimes that it was her fault. She used to wish that her mummy could be happy like other children's mummies. She used to wish that she could have a daddy like other children, to help her look after mummy.'

I perceive a slow tingling nausea creeping through my body.

'When?' I ask, unable to find any other words.

'Three weeks ago,' she says. 'Breast cancer. Are you going to fetch that drink and biscuit?'

So Kate is dead. Beautiful Kate is dead. I've rarely thought of her since I left. We were from different worlds. I had no choice. Suddenly, I feel old and helpless. And what's more, I'm a grandfather at forty three. In fact, it seems I've been a grandfather for the last four years!

'We didn't know what to do,' continues Becky. 'Then I remembered Grandad. What had happened to dear old forgotten Grandad? So I used my detective skills to find him. And here we are.'

I hand Kate a Penguin bar and a drink in a blue Thomas the Tank beaker.

'I've my own family, Rebecca, I can't just...'

'Yes, Morgan, what a lovely name. I was so worried that it would be some unpronounceable Welsh name. And isn't it great that they're about the same age? They can be such friends and comfort to each other growing up – uncle and niece.' She chuckles. A forced, artificial chuckle.

'No, this is ridiculous, you can't just turn up here and...'

A part of me, an unpleasant but substantial part of me, wants to tell her to fuck off out of my life and leave me alone.

Rebecca, Becky, my daughter, indicates for me to keep my voice down in front of Kate.

'Go and play over there a moment, Kate,' she says. Kate obediently ambles to the corner with the toys and inspects what's in the boxes. She's a little splash of pink in a sea of blue.

'It might only be for a while,' says Becky, in an undertone, 'just while I get my head sorted out. I need some Becky time. I need a chance as well. It's about time you did your fair share, don't you think?'

'I can't do it, I don't know her,' I protest. 'I don't know you.'

'But I know you. A little. Like every good detective, I've been watching you for a week now. From a distance. You're a good dad. I would have really liked you for a dad. Maybe things would have been different then. Maybe I wouldn't have ended up like I am now. But it wasn't to be. Perhaps there's still hope for Kate. With her Grampy, she'll get all the things I can't give her. She'll have a future – a chance to break the cycle.'

'You can't just abandon your daughter,' I say. 'What sort of mother does that? And what about the father?'

'Ah, the father... a very good question. What about the father? What does happen to fathers?' She glares at me, unblinkingly. 'And as for me, I guess it must be in the genes. What does that poem say, *they fuck you up, your mum and dad*?'

I'm about to reply when Kate comes pedalling up in Morgan's little car. For the first time since she arrived, there is the hint of a smile on her face.

'Mummy, Mummy, there are lots and lots of toys over there, come and see.'

'Not now, darling, Mummy's got to go away for a while. Grampy will look after you and make sure you have everything you need.' She squats down to kiss little Kate and give her a hug. 'Goodbye, darling, and be a good girl for Grampy.'

With that, she grabs my hand and marches me into the hall. Until now my daughter has betrayed no emotion, but I see the mask slip a little. Is the composure fading?

'These are her things,' she says, pointing at a suitcase she's left in the hall. 'There's a letter in there telling you all the things you need to know and all the paper work you'll need.'

I listen in a confused haze, trying to make sense of things.

'When are you...?'

She shrugs. 'Maybe soon, maybe not. However long it takes.'

'Where are you going? How can I get hold of you?' It strikes me that I don't even know my daughter's surname.

Becky holds my hand in hers and looks me straight in the eyes with those whirlpool eyes of hers – those same pleading, beseeching eyes that bewitched her mother into bed, into carelessly making love without the necessary precautions.

'Take care of her,' she says. Then she walks to her car and drives away.

I watch her leave. I watch her disappear as quickly as she arrived. She doesn't even look behind her to see what she's left behind.

As she turns out of the street, she passes a car coming the other way. It's my wife returning for our romantic night together. Returning for her special birthday surprise.

Growing Apart

We didn't notice it at first. Some of us don't notice these things if they're not relevant, and it wasn't relevant. We only have eyes for our computer screens, our in-trays and out-trays, our desk-tidies and diaries. These things are relevant. We're a little blinkered. It's just the way we are.

It must already have been late afternoon when someone asked out of the blue, *what the hell is that?* Was it Laura who asked? It must have been Laura. If anybody would notice, then Laura would notice.

'What the hell is what, Laura?' we said.

'What the hell is that thing over there?' she said, 'by the window?'

We followed the line of her finger to the windowsill, and that was when we first became aware of its presence. A little green rubbery object in an over-sized plastic pot. We felt sure we hadn't seen it there before.

'It looks like a plant,' we said.

'I know it's a plant,' said Laura, 'but what's it doing there? Where did it come from?'

We stared at the plant and we pondered. We were puzzled. We didn't know what it was doing there or where it had come from. It was a mystery.

William coughed. We turned to look at him.

'If you must know,' he said, 'I put it there and, as I'm sure you're all aware, it is in fact a cactus.'

We were surprised. We were surprised because William rarely spoke unless he was spoken to. And, in all the years he'd been here, William had never brought anything into the office. He didn't have any belongings or keepsakes on his desk. Nothing personal at all.

'You didn't tell us you were bringing in a shrub, William,' we said.

'It's a cactus not a shrub, and I'm telling you now.'

We stared at William, open-mouthed. He'd brought a shrub into the office and placed it on the windowsill without telling us. Without asking us.

'Did your wife give it to you?' we asked.

'More likely she's thrown the miserable-looking specimen out of the house,' said somebody. 'Can't you find somewhere less visible to put it - like the wastepaper basket for instance?'

They had a point. It wasn't the most impressive looking bit of vegetation we'd ever seen. It was just a solitary prickly stump with no offshoots or branches.

William bristled.

'That's because you are a bunch of philistines who don't recognise something beautiful when they see it. The cactus is mine and I have no intention of moving it. I like it just where it is.'

He paused. A few of us made faces behind his back. Then William added, 'and for your information, Marian is no longer.'

William turned and left the room, leaving the statement behind like a lit firework.

We looked at each other awkwardly for some clarification of the words. It was obvious that no one knew what they meant. We were confused. What had happened to Marian? Usually we know everything about everyone else's personal lives. How come we knew nothing about this? We turned to the cactus as if it might tender some sort of explanation.

The stunted desert plant squatted belligerently on the windowsill, silently soaking up the sun's rays. It proffered no explanation.

*

Over the following weeks, William devoted himself diligently to the care of his plant. Each morning, on arrival, he'd feed it with some special concoction of nutrients he brought from home. During the day, he'd regularly shift its position to maximise the sunlight it received. He carried out these duties solemnly, as if he were making offerings to a shrine. A few of us remarked that it was a pity William did not apply the same level of assiduousness to his official office chores and responsibilities.

While the few other plants we had in the office – a spindly old spider plant on a filing cabinet and a rather tatty geranium on Rhiannon's desk - wilted and died with neglect, the cactus thrived. Within a couple of weeks it had doubled in size and still it grew and grew, thrusting ever upwards until it protruded from the window ledge like an organic monolith. We joked that William had missed his vocation, that he should have been a gardener or a farmer. But to tell the truth, we cared little for it. We didn't find it very interesting. We thought it ugly and boring.

Then one day, after the Christmas party, when we had all probably drunk too much, we returned to the office a little tipsy. The office seemed drab and dull to us, so we decided it would be fun to wrap some tinsel around the cactus. Make it look a bit more festive. Phil even made a little paper fairy which he sellotaped to a cocktail stick and stuck into the plant's crown. We chuckled at the cactus in its trimmings. We had been drinking and we were easily amused.

When William walked into the office, we giggled some more.

'What do you think of our Christmas tree, William? Isn't it cute?' we said.

William looked at the plant, but he didn't smile. He marched over to the cactus, seized the cocktail-stick fairy and removed the tinsel. He scrunched them up and deposited them in the bin.

'He's a cactus, not a Christmas tree,' he said.

We looked on in bemusement. What a Scrooge, we thought.

Phil retrieved the crumpled fairy from the bin and declared that, in his view, William had lost his sense of humour. None of us could disagree.

'Thank you for your helpful comments and feedback,' said William. 'Duly noted. Now if you don't mind, and you've quite finished having your bit of fun, I have some work to do.'

What a party-pooper, we thought.

We were about to leave when Dave spoke. Dave was straddling a chair in the corner with a can of lager still in his hand.

'You called the thing a *he*?' said Dave. 'How do you know it's a *he*?'

This was a good question. We were intrigued. We wanted to know the answer.

William said nothing, so Dave persevered.

'I bet you've got a name for it as well, eh?'

William blushed, but still he didn't take the bait.

'In that case,' said Dave, 'I'm going to christen it Colin. Colin the Cactus. Hello Colin my old mate,' he said. 'fancy a little drink?'

Some of us sniggered. We liked Dave. Everybody liked Dave. He was a funny guy.

William glared at us. 'He's called Ben not Colin, and no, he doesn't want a drink.'

We held our hands over our mouths. We were astonished.

'Ben!' snorted Dave, his face contorted with mirth. We knew it was the alcohol, and it was childish, but we began laughing too.

'In that case, I reckon old Ben could do with a drink. He seems a bit tense and uptight to me.' Dave walked over to the plant and dangled the can at an angle above the cactus. He was just messing about. It was entertaining and funny.

'Don't you dare!' threatened William, flushing now to a deep scarlet.

But Dave was enjoying his little prank.

'Surely he's allowed a wee drop at Christmas, even if he isn't allowed to dress up?' Dave said this in a strange voice. We thought it was probably meant to be a Scottish accent. Dave is a bit of a comedian.

Slowly, Dave tilted the can, emptying a stream of amber liquid over the dry prickly exterior of the plant.

William exploded from his chair, grabbed Dave by the throat, and proceeded to throttle him before any of us could do or say anything. Dave gasped, his face turning purple and his arms flailing wildly. Quickly we surmised that this wasn't horseplay, yet we remained frozen to the spot, too shocked to move. We'd never seen William like this before. Eventually, someone moved to prise William from Dave's windpipe. Dave slunk to the floor, his eyes streaming, gulping for breath. William was standing over him, quaking and panting.

'Don't you ever touch him again, do you understand?' he snarled.

We all motioned that we understood, although it was obvious from everybody's expression that no one really understood.

We watched as William picked up his cactus. We watched him caress the pot in his hands and wipe it delicately with a handkerchief from his pocket, then tenderly dab the lager from the plant's spikey flesh. Behind us, Dave cursed and growled, calling William a bloody madman. We dragged Dave away to the bathroom, leaving William and Ben alone.

*

We tried to laugh the incident off, but the atmosphere wasn't the same after that. In the stifling confines of our poorly ventilated office we became tetchy and humourless. Only the cactus seemed truly content in this environment, basking in the heat from the radiator below, greedily inhaling the carbon-dioxide.

William had always been rather quiet and grumpy, but he retreated into himself further, sitting at his desk in silence, brooding. He used to take such pride in his appearance, but we noticed now that his shirts were often creased or stained and buttons were left undone. He shaved irregularly, and his complexion became pale and drawn. There was an unpleasant odour around him, like rotting compost.

Each of us was itching to ask him about Marian, but nobody dared. We were worried he might turn into a raging maniac once again. So we left him alone and tendered our own theories while waiting for the kettle to boil or the microwave to ping. Nobody could blame her if she had left him.

Nevertheless, we worried about William. We urged him to snap out of it, to pull himself together, to get a grip. We didn't like the new William; we wanted the old one back. He was shrivelling away in front of us. And the more he shrank and withered before our eyes, the more the plant bulged in its pot, growing higher and stronger every day.

We glared at the towering imposter silhouetted against the window. The plant stood tall and erect, eclipsing the light, its long shadow stretching across the desks like a dark phallic shroud.

*

One Monday in the New Year, when we arrived in the office, we sensed that something was not right. Something was different. Then we saw it. Ben was slumped lifelessly in his pot. We gathered around the prostrate cactus and stared at it. We looked around at each other with suspicious and accusing glances, but none of us owned up to having done anything. The truth is, many of us felt guilty, hadn't we all called it names? Hadn't we all emptied our cold tea and dregs of coffee into the pot? In a way, we were all culpable.

Fortunately, William wasn't in yet. He'd been coming in later and later and leaving earlier. We didn't like to think what his flexi-time balance was like. We wondered what we would say to him. We searched for words.

When William finally arrived, we confronted him at the office door. We fixed our serious and sombre expressions. William met our gazes. Some of us coughed nervously, and one or two looked away. We were uneasy. You could see that he saw it in our eyes. You could sense that he knew. Withot speaking, we parted to reveal the drooping carcass of the cactus in the window. Nobody spoke as he walked between us to the cactus.

William stood motionless over the pot, as if rooted to the spot. A thick tear oozed like sap from the corner of his eye. We hesitated, each still searching for something to say. Somebody whispered, *Poor Ben.* It wasn't clear which one of us had said it, but it seemed like the right thing to say. So we turned, made our excuses, and shuffled away. Hearing his sobbing, we glanced back. Silently, we watched as his tears fell like kisses into the dry, dead earth.

Exposure

Sion experiences a strange sense of weightlessness, as if he were floating through Space. It's a very pleasant sensation. He stretches his limbs and exhales softly, luxuriating in his dream. But when he snuggles into his pillow, his pillow isn't there. Instead, he bangs his head hard against something solid.

Sion opens his eyes and rubs his scalp. To his surprise he is not in his bed, hence there is no pillow. He seems to be in a large bare cupboard or closet. This is odd, but Sion is far too tired to engage with this information right now. He just wants to resume the dream. He can't quite remember what it was about, but he was content and relaxed when dreaming.

There's a sudden jolt. It feels now like the closet is flying. Is he back in the dream? He can taste bile from his stomach. He thrusts the palms of his hands hard against the floor to balance himself. It feels solid enough. Real enough.

He looks around, squinting through the darkness. On the wall opposite, he can make out a rectangular panel with numbers on it and he realises where he is. He's not in a cupboard or a closet, he's in a lift. A moving lift. That explains the sense of weightlessness. He's not sure whether he's going up or going down or how he came to be here, but he's definitely in a lift. Okay, this is a bit weird, but it's still not particularly interesting to him. There's no reason why he can't shut his eyes again for a few moments more and return to his reveries.

But there is something else that strikes him as odd, that just doesn't feel right. Something is missing. Then he grasps what it is - it's his clothes. He's in a lift and he's naked. Suddenly, Sion is wide awake.

Thoughts panic and collide in a traffic jam of uncertainties. A bolero of questions builds rapidly to a crescendo in his head: *How did he get here? Where is he going? What will happen when the lift stops? Can he be arrested for indecent exposure?* Good questions. Obvious questions, but good ones, nonetheless. And also, *why is he naked in a lift*? Bloody good question.

Answer? He doesn't know, but he'd better come up with something pretty damned quick. Sion needs a story, and he needs it now.

Okay, how's this for an explanation?... somebody stole his clothes!

Hmm, *who stole his clothes? How did they steal them?*

Well, perhaps it was like this: he'd laid down for a moment in the sunshine and..., you know how it is. We've all done it, right? Indulged in a bit of clandestine naturism, when the opportunity arises. Escaped the prison of our garments for a few brief moments so we can savour that liberating sensation of warm sunlight caressing our sun-starved flesh and the soft tickle of the wind as it wafts through our secret nooks and crannies. So we find a quiet little spot, strip off, shut our eyes and before we know it, we're drifting into the land of nod; somewhere peaceful and far away. Only this time, when Sion was dozing, some despicable little snot-rag must have sneaked up and nabbed his clothes. There's no shame in that. It could happen to anyone.

He considers this explanation. Does it make sense? Are there any obvious flaws in this account?

Well, for a start, he has no idea where he is or what time it is. Maybe there isn't any sunshine. It could be raining outside. He presumes he's still in Wales, so it probably is raining. It's not very likely to be sunny and warm. It might even be winter, for all he knows. Or night time! And aren't lifts usually located in offices or shops, not the obvious place for a cheeky bit of nude sunbathing. It occurs to Sion that he hasn't got the foggiest idea about anything. *How did he get into the lift naked?*

Okay, that's the key question. He needs to focus on that. How the hell did he get to where he is now without wearing any clothes?

Someone must have mugged him. Yes, that's it! Somebody attacked him and stole all his clothes because... because they liked his get-up. Envy, pure and simple. Sion is a man of style. A smart dresser. Some scruffy scoundrel must have seen him looking pretty dapper in his trendy gear, sneaked up behind him, and whacked him over the head. Then they stripped him and nicked his money and clothes while he lay unconscious. That could be it. He'd been assaulted!

Or... perhaps somebody had taken his clothes because they wanted to stop him following them? Maybe Sion had stumbled on a crime, or something a little shady. That would sound plausible, and quite heroic. It would make Sion an innocent victim who was standing up against criminals. A have-a-go hero. No issues around incompetency or exhibitionism with that. They can't arrest him for that, can they?

Sion scrutinises his body for injuries or bruises. He doesn't seem to have any marks on him. No physical evidence of an assault. No sore head or anything. And, to be honest, he doesn't recall being attacked. Then again, he doesn't recall anything at all. Perhaps he's got that thing where you get a blow over the head and you forget things. He can't even remember the word, so he may be on to something here. Mind you, he's always forgetting words or mixing words up so he can't bank on that piece of evidence. And the crime? What crime did he see? Who attacked him? Where did it happen? When did it happen? So many questions to consider. Too many questions.

Fortunately, the lift seems to be descending, or ascending, extremely slowly. There's still time for Sion to get his story together. He's a writer for Christ's sake, he must be able to pitch a credible story. He just needs to think it through clearly.

In the films there's always an escape hatch in the lift's ceiling. Maybe he could try to climb out that way and hide there until he comes up with a better plan. That would buy him some time. Sion peers up. He can't see the outline of a hatch. How can he get up there to check it out? There's nothing to stand on. And now that he thinks about it, does he really want to be perched on top of an elevator in a cold dark lift shaft for God-knows how long? He's scared of heights for a start. And what if it goes up to the top and he gets squashed flat like a spikeless hedgehog? No, that's not a good plan at all.

Sion scans his surroundings for other options.

Fuck! He's not alone in here!

An emaciated phantom is in the corner staring at him. Heart pounding, he flings his arm up to defend himself. The pale spook does the same. Sion crouches back into the corner. The spook copies him. Sion relaxes and sighs. It's just his bloody reflection. There's a narrow mirror on the wall behind him, that's all.

He studies the ghostly figure in front of him, squatting like a caged animal in the gloomy confines of the lift. Hey, so what if he's naked? Everyone's the same under their clothes. Why can't he just walk out of the lift starkers, as if it's the most natural thing in the world? Clothing is no more than a social construct. It's other peoples' problem if they're uncomfortable with seeing him in the altogether. He should stride out of the lift upright and proud and dare anybody to challenge his nudity. People won't, they're too polite. They might stare and giggle and whisper to their friends and partners, maybe take a few sly photos with their phones, but no one will actually stop him or ring the police, will they?

And what has he got to be ashamed of? Sion examines his profile in the mirror. Okay, he's no Adonis, but it's a passably normal body, isn't it? Or is it? Are things in the proportion they should be? They're not in the proportion he'd like them to be, that's true. He'd like people to believe that his clothes hid a slightly more impressive physique, but things are sort of in the right place, aren't they? Now he looks a little closer, things do seem a bit dimpled and shrivelled. He crosses his legs. He needs to come up with something else – quickly!

Sion thinks hard. Then it occurs to him; Amnesia, that's the word. Momentarily he rejoices in the recollection. His faculties are returning. Any moment now he will remember what happened. He strains his mind, but there is nothing there. Just blank space.

So how about a stag night? That's more acceptable. He's on his Stag night. Or Stag day. Whatever. His mates stripped him as a prank. These things happen all the time on stags. It's just young lads having a bit of fun. High jinx. Hey, perhaps it really is his stag do. Sion tries to think which mates might have done this to him, but none come readily to mind. And who would he be marrying? The last girl he remembers courting was Carys, but he's sure she ran off with a tattooed boy from Birkenhead a few years ago. He doesn't remember anyone since. Still, no one else needs to know that he's not actually getting married. It's none of their business. But then again, does he want them asking the questions, sticking their mucky fingers into his past and his private life? Nothing good will come of that.

So, what other options has he got? Perhaps he just got up this morning and forgot to get dressed. That's easy enough to do, isn't it? Sion's sure he could do that. He's a bit absent-minded and easily distracted. But how would he have got this far before noticing or being noticed? He doesn't know how far this is, but it certainly isn't anywhere near where he lives. There are no buildings with lifts in the vicinity of his house.

Unless, that is, he was staying in a hotel. In which case, perhaps he'd just got horribly drunk and... well, here he is. Perhaps he's still drunk? Sion considers this. He doesn't feel hungover and his breath seems clear, so this seems unlikely.

Sleep-walking! Of course, that's it. He must have been sleep-walking. He's never done it before, but that could explain it, couldn't it? If he keeps his eyes pretend-closed and his arms out in front of him as if he's in a trance, they'll all think he's some poor bugger who's sleep-walking. Or who's been hypnotised. He can then saunter out of the building and off home like some naked zombie with his willy flopping around in the breeze. Not a lot of dignity in that admittedly, but he may have gone beyond dignity.

Sion senses the lift slowing. He needs to decide on his story. Get the narrative straight. Cover all the bases. Answer every question so that it all makes perfect sense. So that it's coherent and believable. So that it doesn't seem like the made up nonsense of a deluded exhibitionist. An exhibitionist who's got nothing worth exhibiting.

So who is he? What is his character? Is there a cohesive plot to explain the circumstances? Has it got a beginning, a middle and an end? Is it believable?

Writers make things up all the time. They tell lies. That's what they do. Use fancy words and tell lies. Hey, he can say that he was doing it for a story. It was research... for his novel. It's like method acting. He's writing a story about a man who wakes up naked in a lift and he wants to see how people respond and react. He's meticulous in his quest for authenticity. So it's the character that's actually naked, not Sion. He's just immersing himself in the role. Ergo, it's not Sion that's weird, it's the character. Sion would never wander around in public stark bollock naked, you don't have to worry about that. He's a normal guy. So, now that's all clear, he'll be on his way then.

Does this sound convincing? All he'd have to do is go home and write a story about a man waking up naked in a lift, to back up his explanation. He can do that!

Which of these stories to go for? Which one is the most credible? At least one of them must be true... unless? He doesn't want to contemplate the final possible explanation. Could he have mistaken the lift for the shower, leaving his clothes in a neat pile on the carpet outside the lift door on whatever level he got in? Has he done it before? Maybe he does it every bloody day, only he's forgotten. He contemplates the pitying faces staring at him as he stammers his apologies while the police officers and nurses guide him back to his room. No, that only happens to old people, or mad people. Sion isn't old or mad. He's perfectly fine. He's as sane as the next man. Isn't he?

The lift judders to a halt. It's time to decide on the story. Whatever happens, things will be different from now on. Before he got into the lift he was just plain, dull, anonymous Sion. From now on he will be Sion, the man who rides naked in lifts. The doors creak open. He takes a deep breath and steps out. Through the dazzling glare of spotlights he can just make out the banks of cameras pointed his way, as the microphones are thrust into his face.

The Last Knight

The doctor sounds very young over the phone.

'I'm sorry you couldn't be here, by her side... because of the situation with the virus. But our nurses were with her all the time, holding her hand, right to the end. It was peaceful and painless. She had the best possible care, I assure you.'

I take a deep breath.

'Did she say anything...? before...?'

'Well, she did say something. She was actually on ward B2, but she kept insisting that she wanted to spend her last night on C2. She was a bit confused. The drugs can have that effect.'

After the phone call I walk into the lounge, the room that had been her bedroom for the last month, when she could no longer make the stairs. My footsteps echo on the floor.

The duvet and pillows are still draped across the sofa. The glass of water and jars of pills remain on the coffee table next to the chessboard, the game unfinished. To keep her mind agile she liked to play, when she was well enough and lucid, resting between each move.

I study the board. It was inevitable, I suppose. I pick up her remaining knight and move it to square C2.

Check!

Now, if I move my king, she takes my queen. Without my queen, it's check-mate in three moves. Nothing I can do about it. It's finished.

I flick my king over and sweep the pieces away.

Moonhorses

Each night without fail they came, appearing silently out of the blackness like ghosts. Trampling over bracken and sedge they worried at the cold earth, tossing their manes and whinnying gently, as if fearing to wake the dead. You could feel their skittish dancing hooves pulsing through the saturated mountain soil. Even in the dark depths of winter they returned, pounding at the freezing layers of snow until wet pools of soft brown mulch blossomed from beneath the dense white gag that smothered the land. When others had forgotten, when others had abandoned me, the horses remained, loyal as pilgrims.

These are the Moonhorses. They are the guardians of these desolate limestone ridges. Hidden away from the world of people and machines the wild Moonhorses trek their ancient pathways, oblivious to the hum and glare of the streetlights shimmering in the valleys below. They are my confidantes. My dreamcatchers. I always thrill to see them.

The horses have always been with me. In my dreams. Ever since I was a little girl. Ever since I opened the door one New Year's Eve when I was six years old to a grinning horse's skull demanding my money. Then they were frightening. I called them my 'night-mares'. They haunted me like a galloping apocalypse with teeth bared and gleaming, their black cavity eyes penetrating deep into the soft tissue of my soul. I'd wake up screaming in terror: '*Please Mummy, don't let the horses get me! Daddy, Daddy, take the horses away!*'

Soon after that they came and took Daddy away. He never came back.

In time, the dreams became less frequent and more benign. Like all girls, I wanted my own pony more than anything; to feed and to groom, to coax and to straddle. To fix my feet high in the stirrups and feel the wind in my hair. To clench its supple muscular back between my thighs, rippling and swaying with every twitch and tug of the reigns.

But in my world, the girls didn't own horses. There were no green fields and gymkhanas, only rows and rows of dreary dead-end streets that stretched like lines of gravestones along the valley floor. It was a world of hand-me-down Barbie dolls and prams; of stilettos and glitter and smoking weed behind the Welfare. That was my world, and I never wanted to be part of it. I didn't belong there.

Once I was old enough, I would escape on Saturday afternoons to the farm at the end of Pen-rhiw Lane and peer over the fence at the sombre horses eating their hay alone in the stables. When I thought no one was looking I crept across the yard, to feed them apples or lumps of sugar and run my fingers through their manes, stroking their long lean faces. And I'd talk to them.

I didn't know then that he'd been watching me: the Whispering Man. He liked to listen to me talking to them. He told me it was okay. He could tell that they liked me. I was so gentle and soft, he said. He told me that horses were clever and that they absorb every word; I could tell them anything and they'd understand. So I whispered stories to them the way the man had showed me. I told them my secrets, shared my dreams with them. I believed that behind those sad dark eyes, they were listening to me. They trusted me, and I trusted them. I had an affinity with horses that I never had with people.

But those weren't the Moonhorses. My bloodsisters. The ones that stand now mutely, leaning over the loose cordon of red and white tape that flaps mournfully in the breeze like a lost soul. The ones that impassively scrutinise the men and women coming and going from beneath the tarpaulin, swishing their tales as the trespassers defile their land.

My wild scraggy companions didn't show up until later, until I was no longer a girl and only just a woman. They first appeared one evening in June last year, a night I will always remember.

A cool breeze blows through the valley and the clouds billow menacingly above the Bryn. I watch the swallows swoop and dive around the outbuildings, then come to rest along the telephone lines. From a distance they look like little flying crotchets and quavers arranging themselves into different tunes. Somewhere a dog is barking, but everything else is quiet and still. There are no signs or sounds, yet I know he is here. I can sense his eyes on me.

A light drizzle begins to fall. It's late. I should go back home, but for some reason I stay, unable to turn around. My fingers are tense and clammy. A pebble scuttles across the yard behind me and a shadow slides silently under my feet. I shudder as I feel the warm vapour of his breath creep across the nape of my neck.

The Whispering Man strokes my hair and tells me not to be afraid. He says that I should trust him. He's been waiting and waiting and he cannot wait any longer. He runs his fingers down my cheek, and his voice is soothing and reassuring. Did I know that I was beautiful?

He clutches my mouth roughly between his hands and kisses me. His breath stinks of tobacco and stale alcohol. He seizes my wrist. I shouldn't be so nervous and skittish, like a foal. I'm a woman now, not a girl. There is no harm in touching. He puts his other hand upon my breast and he tells me not to scream; it will spook the horses. Anyway, nobody will hear me, so there is no point in being difficult. No one else knows and no one else cares. We are alone. It is just him and me.

The man leads me to the barn and presses me down against the hay. He forces his hands over me. Makes my hands touch him.

'It's easy,' he says. 'I am the stallion and you are the mare. A pretty, pretty little mare. So soft and white and gentle.'

He pushes my head down on to him, groaning and whispering, calling me names. Horrible names. I gag and stumble and retch, and the whispering becomes a snarl. He is angry now. He wrenches my hair and rips at my clothes. I spit and scratch and bite and flail against his fists, but he is too strong. He has so much hatred in his eyes and I don't know why. He says that I am to blame, that it's all my fault. Then he does things to me; hurts me. Over and over again, whispering filthy things in my ears. I plead and I whimper and I beg, but I have ceased to be human to him. My eyes swell and spoil under the blows until his face blurs and pixelates and I can no longer see him, or feel him. I am sinking. I am drowning. Only his whispering, like water, fills my ears. The last thing I remember is I'm floating high above. I can see him squatting above me, his body an angry, pumping fury. I am still beneath him, my face a mask. Bloody red blotches sprout like poppies in the straw. Then there is nothing; only darkness and the sound of pounding hooves fading into the distance.

That night I saw them for the first time; the Moonhorses. I'll never forget them. However hard I try, I'll never forget. From behind the blurred frame of his sodden face the moon unexpectedly appeared, and there they were, six fretting equine heads rearing up through the swirling mist, their nostrils flaring. They emerged out of the gloom in the driving rain like an apparition, a looming shadow silhouetted against the horizon. I thought they were angels at first. I really did. I thought they'd come to claim me. I saw the fear in his eyes. For a moment I believed they'd save me, but they were no match for the Whispering Man. They kept a distance when he cursed and swung his shovel at them. They stood and watched and stamped, whinnying restlessly. The raindrops dripping from their forelocks looked like beads of silver tears in the moonlight.

Perhaps they were angels. Perhaps it was just too late. Perhaps they saw the broken bundle of bound white flesh and the steady scarlet trickle dribbling into the bleached grey podsol, and they knew they were too late. There was nothing they could do now. Just keep a vigil. Bear witness as the man cut his scar into their land. Listen, as the stifled screams subsided, as the gasping lungs fell silent, as the last writhing breath stilled. Watch as the man kicked the bloodied little rag doll into the shallow puddle trench. Watch as I curled up forever on my bed of seashells and coral and petrified plankton. As the soil fell finally over my eyes and I sank into the womb of the mountain, foetal and fossil.

It's taken them nine months to find me. I was an unsolved mystery. A statistic. Another missing person vanished into thin air. So few people pass this way; the occasional rambler straying from the beaten tracks and paths, some forestry workers on the slopes below, but no one else. Once, a man set up his camp by the stream. He almost found me. In the night he weed onto my grave. You could tell he was frightened in the darkness. He could sense he was not alone.

I thought I would be here forever, anonymous and forgotten, but the snows thawed and the spring rains that followed washed away the thin loose soil. Then one night, two weeks ago, I stuck my bony finger and scalp through the surface of the land again. They emerged on the barren lime moorland like pure white snowdrops. Beneath them, my eyes stared out from the soil into the April sunlight until the crows and buzzards came and picked away at the rotting fragments of flesh that had clung through the cold, damp winter. Soon, only the cleansed bones and sockets remained, floating in a shallow sea of soil between the mountain and the stars. And that is how they found me, washed up like flotsam on a desolate Welsh hillside.

In truth, I didn't want them to find me. It's quiet here. The air is fresh and my faithful companions are never far away. On a clear day you can see right across the valley to the hills beyond. You can almost see the old house huddled in the shadows between the uplands. But I do not yearn to return to that life. Even with lungs, I never truly breathed down there. This is where I belong.

And you know, that isn't me they're digging up. Not really. That's just a shell. A pile of old shells that used to hold my life; that used to breathe. Now I've become the breath. I've leached into the landscape. I'm swimming with the dolphins through the trees. I'm soaring with the buzzards above the clouds. I'm galloping with the horses through your dreams.

Smoke gets in your Eyes

Cardiff General Station, 1956. All is motion. Steam billows, pistons roar, coal trucks rumble and screech over points. People swarm around a locomotive on the platform like ants around a helpless centipede.

In an office behind one of the platforms, Gwyn, a young clerk from the Rhondda, glances up at the large Great Western company clock on the wall. It's five past twelve. Hurriedly, he dabs the nib of his pen in the blotting paper, closes his book of accounts and gets up to leave. He puts on his jacket and strides out into the crisp autumnal sunlight.

Gwyn is going to meet Lucy. This is their first date, and he's late. Can you call it a date? They're not really courting, but... was he mistaken about that twinkle in her eyes when she smiled back at him and said, 'yes of course, Gwyn, I'd love to meet you for lunch. Shall we say twelve at Astey's?'

Outside the entrance to the café, Gwyn catches his own reflection in the window and winks appreciatively. He's looking dapper with his short coal-black hair brylcreamed into a fashionable quiff, a young man in his prime with his whole life in front of him. He stands on the threshold and peeks through the glass.

Lucy is sitting by herself in a little alcove on the far side. She is staring into a small hand mirror, carefully applying or adjusting her lipstick. She still has her coat on. There is something so self-composed and vibrant in her movements. It's like peering through goggles into a deep ocean at a creature that he's never observed before. She looks up in his direction, but she does not see him behind the glass. Her brow crinkles with doubt and she bites her lower lip as she scours the entrance for her date. Now she seems vulnerable and fragile. So vulnerable and fragile and beautiful that a wave of yearning ripples through him and he actually shudders. He wants to rush in and tell her not to worry. Hold her in his arms and tell her that everything will be alright. He wonders if she is the one. If this prim little Cardiff girl with the bob of curly brown hair will be the one for him. And is he the one for her?

Gwyn rakes his fingers through his hair, inhales deeply and takes the plunge through the door and into the café. Through the door, and into the future.

*

A cool breeze blows in across the Bay. I shiver and tighten my collar to keep out the icy tentacles of the south-westerly. Dad, as usual, doesn't flinch. He stands motionless, breathing in the view in slow, gasping gulps.

'A bit different from how it used to look,' I venture.

'Aye.'

'Big improvement on the old docks, don't you think?'

'If you like this sort of thing,' he says.

Dad does like this sort of thing, but he won't admit it. If this was a Mediterranean resort or any other place in the world than Wales, then this would be his sort of thing and his sort of place. But because this is Cardiff and his patch and his son he's talking to, he can't bring himself to credit this. Approval is conditional. Praise is grudging. All change is bad. It's just how things are.

I've driven them down here. Him and Mam. Gwyn and Lucy. Thought it would do them good to get out of the house now that Dad has lost his licence. Because of the glaucoma.

'Will you do the test again?' I ask.

He shrugs.

'But your sight's fine. Why don't you give it another shot?'

'You try telling the DVLA that. As far as they're concerned I'm crocked and that's that.'

'But what about the shopping, and visiting the hospital with Mam?'

'Oh, we'll get by. There is such a thing as public transport, you know.' He smiles, but it looks more like a grimace. I know there is no point arguing with him, the stubborn old mule that he is.

'I'm going to have to give up the allotment though,' he says, 'at least until your mam's feeling better.'

The allotment has been his pride and joy for the last twenty years and mam will not get better. We both know that.

I look down at Mam. She seems so cosy, wrapped snug in her blankets, staring out over the water, lost in her own world. She resembles a shrivelled King Canute sat on his throne, trying to keep the tide at bay. Except, the tide came in long ago, and it's never going back out.

As if she senses us watching her, she calls out something, but the words are taken by the wind. We walk over to her.

'Are you alright, Mam?' I ask.

She looks up at me with wonderment.

'Oh, there you are, love,' she says. 'Look, can you see them all, over there?' She points a bony finger across the water towards the barrage. Her face is lit up with a childish delight.

'See what, Mam?' I ask. 'Do you mean the boats?'

She scowls at me irritably.

'Boats? They're not boats, silly, they're trains. Choo Choo trains.'

I follow her gaze out into her world. A world I cannot see, nor will ever be able to see.

'Come on,' she says, 'hurry up, or we'll miss our train.'

Dad hobbles over.

'Don't worry Lucy, love, we've still got time, it hasn't gone yet.' He takes the handles of the chair and wheels her unsteadily along the waterfront. Mam crunches up her face in the wind and the breeze blows through her hair. For a brief moment she looks like a young girl at the seaside, and I feel a tear well up from somewhere deep inside.

I reach over to brush a frond of hair from her face, and she smiles vacantly at me.

'Don't worry,' she says, 'it's just the smoke, it gets in your eyes.'

The Arbour

Alice pushes away the voices in her head and skips up the lane from the house through a rainbow arcade of primroses and violets and celandines. She hums a medley of nursery rhymes to herself, oblivious to the buzzing galleries of fresh blooms on either side. Behind her, on the patio, her parents sip their tea and finish their breakfast, taking advantage of the early spring sunshine. When they had started to talk about adult things, Alice had supped down her lemon cordial and slipped discreetly away from the table. She was impatient to escape to her special place up on the Rhiw.

Half way up the lane, Alice arrives at a semi-circular wooden structure hidden in a recess on the hillside among a jumble of rhododendrons and laurel. It has an in-laid bench and an open lattice of beams for a roof. Something about its shape reminds Alice of the bow of a longship. This is the Arbour, and it's her favourite place in all the world.

Alice sits on the bench and swings her legs. She contemplates the tree-framed view before her - the vast green expanse stretching to the coast. In the distance, ships glide by on the estuary with imperceptible motion. She can no longer hear the voices that have been haunting her; all she can hear is the wind blowing through the branches overhead and the sound of birdsong all around her. She closes her eyes and imagines she's a buzzard soaring high over the Rhiw, forever and ever and ever.

'Alice! Alice! Where are you?'

Alice jolts awake and opens her eyes wide. She must have drifted off to sleep. The woman's voice is not like the others in her head; it's lucid and close at hand, yet there is nobody to be seen. Alice freezes, holding her breath.

A disembodied face appears from behind a bright pink blossom of rhododendron.

'Oh, we thought we'd find you here. So typical of Alice to disappear during her own party', says the face. 'Craig's got to go. He wishes to say a few words before he leaves, don't you Craig?'

Party? What party? Who is this woman, anyway? The face, now joined by the rest of the body, is familiar, but Alice can't quite place how she knows it. Behind the woman, two smartly dressed young men appear, their features blurred in the sunlight. She isn't sure which one is Craig.

The woman pushes the plumper of the two indistinct young men forward into her sight. Even now she can see his features up close, there remains something plain and unremarkable about his face. For a moment, she thinks he's about to kiss her and she recoils, but then he seems to change his mind and shakes her hand rather formerly instead. This must be Craig. She doesn't think she knows him.

Craig is speaking. 'I just wanted to say, before I left, how much I've enjoyed the party and... well, I was wondering if perhaps you and I, we could, you know... next week sometime,... if you're free?'

Alice is astonished. Behind Craig's back the woman is giving Alice a thumbs-up and an exaggerated wink.

'Yes, yes, I suppose so. Why not?' she replies absently to Craig. 'What party is it?' she asks the woman.

The woman laughs. 'It's your party, you silly-billy. Your twenty-first. I do believe you are a bit squiffy, Alice.'

'My twenty-first birthday?'

'Yes, Alice dearest, you're twenty-one years old today and I think that perhaps you've consumed a little too much of the bubbly. Anyway, Colin and I have some very important news for you, so you're just going to have to glug some more of the stuff. We didn't want to steal your thunder by announcing it to everyone in the party on your special day, but I,... I mean, we've been dying to tell you all day. Colin...'

The woman's voice breaks off and she bites her tongue, obviously excited. The other man steps forward and takes the woman's hand. He is handsome and smiles knowingly at Alice.

'I've asked Margaret to marry me,' he says, '... and she's accepted.'

So this woman is Margaret. Alice doesn't recognise her best friend disguised in this woman's body. She's all grown up. And Colin? He seems familiar too. She senses that there's something important that she needs to say to him, but she can't remember what it is.

'Isn't it just wonderful?' says Margaret. 'Such a perfect day. I think we shall remember this day for the rest of our lives.'

Behind Margaret's head, Alice observes a fluffy white cloud morphing into different shapes: a claw becomes a crocodile, becomes a nameless Mediterranean island.

'Yes, such a perfect day,' says Alice. She tries to recollect which island it is, but the wind has already re-moulded the cloud into a shapeless muddle.

'Are you coming back down to the party, Alice?' asks Margaret. 'We've got some serious celebrating to do.'

Alice's head is spinning. Margaret is right, it must be the champagne.

'I'll be along shortly,' she says, 'I just need some fresh air.'

Such a handsome young man, she thinks, once they've departed. It's glorious to see two young people so obviously in love. They were both so happy that she cannot fathom why she feels so miserable.

The day is hot now and the high sun is casting grid lines of shadow across the floor of the Arbour, dappling her face with sunlight and shade. Alice hitches her dress and stretches her legs, luxuriating in the caress of the sun upon her thighs. She inhales the sweet scent from the honeysuckle draped across the trellis. Distractedly, she reaches down and picks a dandelion that has grown up through one of the slats and pinches each petal off in turn. She chants to herself as she plucks, *he loves me, he loves me not, he loves me, he loves me not,* until only one petal remains: *He loves me not.* She sighs and hurls the mutilated carcass of the dandelion to the floor in disgust. 'Silly flower,' she cries. Alice extends a finger and traces it over the heart carved into the pillar of the Arbour. She mouths to herself the words scratched inside the heart, *'Alice + Colin 4 ever'.*

When Alice turns around she is surprised to see him sitting there, staring out towards the channel. She snuggles up against him, elated that he has found her. Lifting her lips towards his she murmurs, 'I love you, Colin, I always have.'

'I'm not Colin, I'm Craig.'

Startled, Alice looks up and sees that it is indeed Craig; pale and gaunt and dour Craig. What's he doing here, squatting in her secret bower? He doesn't belong here. It should be Colin! Still, Craig is warm and comfortable and solid like his name. She supposes that if she must let someone into her secret place, it may as well be him. She buries her head in his ribs and listens to the slow beat of his heart. It reminds her of the grandfather clock in the foyer of the house, ticking and tocking day after day after day, slower and slower and slower.

Alice is awoken by the shrill alarm of children yelling. A small boy and a girl are squabbling on the path in front of the Arbour, tugging at a scrawny little doll between them.

'Hey! you two, what are you doing here?'

They stop fighting and turn their ruddy faces towards Alice, the doll suspended between them. They look concerned.

'It's only us, Mum. We're your children, remember?'

'My children? Yes, of course, you're my children. I know that,' she says uncertainly. 'Now, what's the problem?'

'Tell her, Mum,' says the boy, 'it's my Action Man, she's not supposed to play with it.'

'He said I could have it and now he just wants to spoil my game,' replies the girl.

Alice considers the information: her children, a doll, an argument. She is vexed. It was so peaceful before they came. She wants a quick resolution to the dispute, but she doesn't know how she should go about it. They are both looking at her expectantly.

'What will your father say?' she says, irritably.

'Dad?' says the little boy, glancing nervously at Craig. 'I don't think he's going to say anything, is he?'

'But he probably would have said that I could have it,' blurts the girl. She wrenches the dangling figure from her brother's grasp and runs off down the path in the direction of the house, hooting loudly. The boy stumbles after her, bawling and cursing.

'Children! Children!' yells Alice, but they've already gone. She tries to remember their names. Perhaps she should go after them and ask them? But it's too late. They've already faded into the distance, far away and out of sight. Alice turns to ask Craig, but he's disappeared too. She is relieved. She brushes the dust from the seat into a clump of wilting forget-me-nots. She is alone. All is tranquil once again.

Alice lights a cigarette, inhales deeply and examines her surroundings. The Arbour is falling into disrepair. She must do something about it. The wooden slats are rotten and a thin crust of lichen and tufts of damp moss swathe the floor. Columns of fungae like overgrown toenails cling to the pillars. Straggling shoots of honeysuckle and bramble intrude through the trellis onto the decking like the outstretched arms of prisoners begging for alms through the bars of their cells. She can hear them whispering all around her: *Let us in! Let us in!*

'Go away,' she implores. 'Please go away and leave me alone. This is my place. No one else shall have it!'

Alice claws desperately at the spindly tendrils of ivy that clutch at the frame of the Arbour. Frantically, she searches for some sign that this is still her domain, but she cannot find the carving she is looking for, the declaration of her undying love for a boy she never even kissed.

Alice collapses onto the bench, weeping, her head in her hands. She lets the cigarette butt fall from her grasp to join the countless others jammed between the ridges of the decking. As she watches its amber embers glow beneath her, a distant memory engulfs her: a memory of thick dark smoke wafting through the trees; of heat and flames; of creaking timber and falling masonry; of sirens and shouting and sobbing. Alice thrusts her hands to her ears and rocks back and forth until the sounds have gone, and all is quiet and still once again.

A cold wind is gusting through the trees. Alice shivers and splutters. The sunlight has vanished; it must be getting late. She should return to the house before the darkness descends. Looking up, she sees that the branches are almost bare except for a few crinkled leaves clinging precariously to the tips of twigs. *'When did that happen?'* she wonders. *'Where did the summer go?'*

Alice grabs her stick and heaves herself wearily to her feet. She's been on the Arbour too long. It's time to return home. She trudges across the soggy carpet of leaves and steps down from the Arbour. She makes her way uneasily back along the path towards the house. It's dusk already. With each shuffling step she takes, her breath wheezes and rattles in her ribs. She strains through the gloom, searching for the familiar profile of the house, but the house is no longer there. It's just an empty husk of blackened stone and rubble. The glassless windows peer blindly out across an untidy jungle of scrub where the garden should be. Rooks rise noisily from the rafters, their cawing echoing eerily through the edifice of the ruin.

Confused, Alice turns back towards the Arbour, but it too has gone, swallowed up by the creeping tentacles of the mountain. Only a single faint light remains in the middle of the undergrowth, where the Arbour should be. From somewhere, she can hear the voices calling her once again. They're saying:

Mum!

Grandma!

Mrs Edwards!

Can you hear us?

Can you understand us?

Do you remember?

She doesn't know where the voices are coming from, or who they are talking to. She wants them to be quiet. To leave her alone on the Rhiw as the light fades and the Arbour disappears finally into the blackness.

Still ill

The sun trailed me all the way back to Wales like a poorly disguised private detective. Every time I glanced in my rear-view mirror, it was there. But when I turned up towards the valley, it skulked away, as if I'd crossed some unseen boundary. As if I'd passed out of its domain.

I park the car in a lay-by high above the Cwm and follow a sheep-track up onto the mountain. It's only once I'm up on the crest of the ridge that I feel the force of the south-westerlies blowing in from the coast, many miles away. I pull my jacket tight and thrust forward into the wind.

On the far edge of the ridge, slabs of sedimentary outcrops jut out above the escarpment. I brush the hair from my eyes and peer down into the bowl of the valley below. It's like looking into a rock-pool. Wispy clouds float over the landscape like fronds of seaweed stirred by an incoming tide, while rows of tiny stone houses limpet-kiss the slopes on either side. A single car scuttles up the hairpin bends towards the Bwlch, its engine churning and straining. Other than this one vehicle, and the sheep, of course, I am totally alone. I breathe in the fresh, dank air. It feels as if I've never been away. I wonder if anyone else will come. If anyone else will remember, after all this time?

Back when we were young, it felt like we were standing on the edge of the world up here. On those rare cloudless days, you can see over the Valleys as far as the sea, and beyond that, more land and the beginnings of another country. Another world. And much further over there to the west, where leaden oceans merge with leaden skies, lay America!

I remember Griff standing here, his arms stretched out into the driving rain, straining his eyes into the distance. He swore that if you concentrated hard enough, you could see Liberty's Torch rising like Excalibur out of the haze. But you had to concentrate really hard. And smoke plenty of dope.

This was our favourite place. Our special place. Where me and Griff would come to escape the world. To be alone and to be together. Up here, we could breathe. Up here, we could dream.

But I haven't come to dream today. I've come to remember. I thought I'd find the exact spot easily, but my memory is playing tricks on me. The location on the plateau edge is etched on my mind like a scar, yet things seem different now, distorted through the prism of time. The topography, the scale, the perspective, none is quite as I remember, as if God has subsequently rearranged the furniture.

Scanning the slabs of sandstone for traces, I find a metal tablet screwed to a boulder. It says:

Stanley and Olive Pugh
Together for Eternity

I'm disorientated. I don't remember ever seeing this before. Momentarily I wonder who they were? What was their story? What was their connection with this barren place?

Then I see it, the spot where it happened. Wilder and more exposed than I remember it, but definitely the place. Cautiously, I clamber down to an overhanging crag. I drop-kick a stone over the edge and watch it spin and fall, bouncing once before disappearing into the scree below.

It's strange coming back here today, after being away so long. We said we'd do this forever. Meet here on this day each year, whatever the weather, wherever we were. To be together and to remember. But it's been more than fifteen years since I last came. Just another one of the fickle promises of youth that I've broken. Beth came dutifully for a few years, but she's married and has children now, so you can't blame her for being unfaithful. People move on. We all change.

And if I never came, why should anyone else?

So I guess this will be the last time. Once I've sorted things out with the old house, there will be no more reasons to return.

Mrs Griffiths rang a few weeks back to offer her condolences to me and Beth. It was kind of her as she hardly knew Mam. She asked about me - what I was doing now? How was life in the big city? Was I still courting? She said she often thought of me. I thanked her and answered politely, but anything I said in reply sounded empty. I wanted to tell her that I thought of her too, and of Griff. How I still think of him often. And miss him, more than anyone could ever know. Even now.

*

Griff was my best butty. From our first day at school we'd been friends. We'd grown up together. 'Griff and Gaz'; we were like brothers. Inseparable.

We used to come up here to lark around and kill time. We'd talk all sorts of nonsense about our hopes and dreams for the future. Dreams about fame, money, cars, girls, sipping ice-cold beers beneath palm trees on tropical islands. All the usual clichés. And always the two of us, together.

And then there were the songs. What we both dreamt of more than anything else was to be in a band, to be up on a stage performing for our adoring fans. It was a silly adolescent fantasy, but we were serious about our music. Really serious. We were going to make it. Sometimes we'd bring our acoustic guitars up here and sit on the ledge and jam, our legs dangling over the side. We'd strum songs we liked and songs we didn't like, practise chords, try out riffs, improvise lyrics and drink cider, basking in the applause of the sheep.

Eventually we formed a band. We drafted Toddy and Rolo in on bass and drums. They were pretty awful to be honest and didn't share our taste in music (they were into metal), but they didn't care and we didn't care. Lloydy was too lazy to learn to play an instrument, so he said he'd be our manager and roadie. We'd meet up at Lloydy's garage where we dossed and thrashed and smoked and plucked and stuffed ourselves on his mother's Welsh Cakes until we finally had some songs. Mostly cover versions, but two or three of our own as well that me and Griff had written. The Dare Devils were born, and for six months we were legend.

It was Lloydy that got us our first gig. Dai and Ceri Hopkins were having a joint eighteenth birthday party at the Institute and said we could play. That first performance was thrilling. Electric. All four of us nervous, excited, a little pissed. We covered The Smiths and The Clash, Iggy and Joy Division. We even played a hammed up ACDC track to keep Toddy and Rolo happy. And we sang a couple of our own songs. It was loud and chaotic and flawed, but nobody cared. Everyone was smashed and happy and they danced and cheered and clapped and whistled and gobbed... and someone spewed on the dance floor. Nobody gave a toss when we messed up. Inside, I was buzzing. Nobody laughed at my ridiculous quiff.

After the gig, everyone came up and said we were awesome, even though most were too pissed to discern if we were any good or not. In truth we were raw and shambolic, but we had something about us. Griff really had something, and we all knew it. Especially him. He turned up that night grinning broadly, his straggling locks dyed a dazzling platinum blonde, wearing eyeliner and mascara. In his shadow, I guess my quiff was not even noticed. Griff was in his element on the stage, at ease in the spotlight, posing and flirting, twisting and gyrating his body in ways I'd never seen him do before. Ripping his shirt open and writhing on the floor as he sang. Everyone loved him, especially the girls.

Griff was amazing, but still it was odd seeing his transformation. He'd done none of these things during rehearsals. Had he planned it all and acted it out in front of the mirror at home beforehand? I felt a sense of unease mixed in with the exhilaration. A sense of something slipping away no sooner than it had arrived. He sang my lyrics, the ones I'd first shared with him up on the mountain, as if they were his own, staring into the eyes of the smartest girl in the sixth form. He never once acknowledged my contribution or turned to look at me.

That spring, me and Griff spent every spare second together, hanging out, listening to music, writing new songs, experimenting with different sounds. We played a few gigs locally and down in Pandy, and we were building up a bit of a local following. But our A level exams were looming, and the future hung over us like a cloud. I'd been offered places at a couple of English Universities. Griff, we both knew, but never mentioned, was struggling in school. He'd been thrown off Geography and was not getting the grades in the other subjects. His parents had split up, and the situation at home was difficult. He despised his dad and was forever having blazing rows with his mother, although she was always really pleasant with me. He still talked about going away to college, but the band and the music meant everything to Griff. School and school work were a distraction, an annoyance. He wouldn't need any mundane qualifications where he was going. His only future was a fantasy.

So Griff spent most of his time at Lloydy's practising in the garage or at my place, up in my bedroom. Bethan would often slink in to watch and listen and we'd try out our new stuff on her. Griff always used to play up to her, thrusting his body or kneeling at her feet to sing a ballad, his face in hers until she blushed and squirmed away. To tell the truth, I was never comfortable with this. All the girls fancied Griff, and Beth was no different. He was my best friend, but I didn't want him going with my sister. I wanted him for myself.

When I think now of those days, what I remember most is his energy and vitality. The life force seemed so strong in him. At that age you feel immortal. You can't comprehend how fragile life is. I never imagined that by the end of that summer, Griff would be dead.

*

One year after his death, on the anniversary, this is where we came. Me, Toddy, Dai and Rolo set off in the afternoon, haversacks laden with cans and flagons of cider, Rolo's camping stove and a stash of weed. Dai had his ghetto-blaster, and I took my guitar. Later in the evening, Bethan came up with Mel (who fancied Toddy) and they brought up marshmallows and candles and fresh flowers. When the pubs shut, Lloydy, who worked behind the bar in the Red Cow, came up with his mate Pickles. Lloydy smuggled up a bottle of Jack Daniels his dad had 'given him' and his mam had made us sandwiches and flasks of tea. He'd picked a few mushrooms up on the golf-course and added them to the brew – to give it 'a little extra kick'. Lloydy's mam always used to make us Welsh Cakes when we went to the house. We'd stuff ourselves on them until we were almost sick. Mrs Lloyd had thought of us this time and made some specially. And thought of Griff, I guess. Like the rest of us, one year on, thinking of Griff.

It was a warm and still summer evening and we sat here through the night, keeping a vigil. We placed a photograph against the rock and made a shrine with the candles. We drank lager and mushroom tea, ate Mrs Lloyd's Welsh Cakes, held hands, sang songs and remembered. Toddy said people driving over the Bwlch would think we were devil worshippers sacrificing a virgin.

We remembered Griff's cheeky smile, all the stupid things he used to say and do, how he never seemed to have a care in the world, although we knew this wasn't true. The others were sad, but none of them had been as close to Griff as me. I sat there, rocking back and forth silently, tears scolding my cheeks.

Toddy and Dai made a fire, and we toasted the marshmallows and huddled together under the stars. After midnight, I picked up my guitar and played some of our favourite songs. My head throbbed and spun. I played *Meet on the ledge* and everyone sang along and cried. I remember that the girls had such sweet voices. Like angels.

I might have been stoned, but I realised why Beth was sitting where she was, and what she was trying to hide. She was the only one I'd told and who understood about the lines scratched into the rock beneath her. The lines carved by Griff, just before he jumped. So when I strummed the chords of *Still ill* I noticed how she shifted her position, spreading herself like a bird protecting its nest. A subtle and deliberate movement. I sensed her eyes on me, all of their eyes scrutinising me. Even the stars were watching me. Through my swollen eyes I scanned the universe above as I sang for some sign that Griff was gazing down and watching too, but all I could see was the vast emptiness of space, all I sensed was nothingness. I got to the chorus and then I snapped. Before anybody could stop me I leapt up and flung the guitar into the abyss, listening to it shatter and echo on the rocks below, and then I was shaking and sobbing, and Toddy was holding me, suddenly sober, telling me not to worry, that everything was going to be alright.

'What the fuck, Gaz? I thought you was going to bloody well jump off too.'

But I didn't jump. Unlike Griff, I'm still here.

And the words are still here. The words Griff carved into the rock. The last words he ever wrote. They're weathered now and barely visible beneath the lichen and moss. But you can still make them out.

*

I rarely saw Griff in the months before he died. I told myself it was the exams. I needed to concentrate. To focus. I was desperate to pass and to escape. To find a way out of the valley and the small-town mentality where everyone knew your name and your business. To get away from the past and make a new start. To get away from Griff.

The last time we talked it was May-day, I remember it vividly. I was angry with him. We'd played a gig on Saturday night. Afterwards he'd started snogging Beth again. I felt betrayed. By him and by her. There was no school that day because of the bank holiday so he'd called round my house in the afternoon. He'd been drinking or had taken something, but he was trying to act sober. The faded mascara could not disguise his bloodshot eyes and ashen pallor.

He wanted to come in. He said he had some ideas for improving the set. He was slurring. I'd been watching TV but told him I was busy and had too much work to do – the first exam was in a fortnight. When he persevered I gave in but said we should go out, even though I felt embarrassed in his company when he was wearing make-up. I needed to get him away from the house, where Beth was.

So we walked the streets and ambled aimlessly up to the picnic site by the forestry. Griff wittered relentlessly about the gig on Saturday; how Toddy had love bites around his nipples from a girl in Year Ten, how Lloydy had stripped to *Reel around the Fountain* and fallen off the stage, and how Moggy had taken his clothes and posted them in the post-box over the road. There were always things like this to mull over, to enjoy again during the following week. This was part of the folklore of youth.

But I wasn't listening to him now. These things didn't seem to matter anymore. The evening was calm and still and there was a shimmering radiance over everything, as if a cosmic aura clung to me and everything around me as we walked. I felt detached from my body and I knew that this moment would stay with me forever, that it was special. Standing on top of a picnic table, I gulped in the aroma of damp pine needles and studied how the dappled sunlight made the shadows of the branches dance. Goose pimples crept over my flesh and an electricity surged through my veins. Something was changing. The world was full of possibilities. I felt young and alive. I felt free, and I felt trapped.

Griff was singing to himself, using a branch for a microphone. He was hamming it up for all it was worth, even though I was his only audience and I really couldn't give a shit. He had no sense of anything wondrous or sacred in that moment. I saw now how pathetic and shallow and self-obsessed he was. The sun and the stars and the Earth were inconsequential, everything revolved around him and his ego and whatever it was that shone out of his arse. I'd had enough. The spell was broken and I could contain myself no longer:

'Did you get off with Beth?' I challenged him. Griff ignored me. He just kept on singing to himself in his thin, whiney voice.

'Did you sleep with Beth?' I asked again, more forcefully this time.

He paused his performance and nonchalantly kicked a pine-cone under one of the tables, avoiding making eye-contact.

'Bethan's a nice kid,' he said.

'Just answer the fucking question, Griff!'

'What's it to you, Ga? You'll be going off to University soon. It won't matter to you what Beth does then or who she sleeps with. Or what I do.'

Griff was repulsive to me at that moment. 'Is that her make-up you're wearing?'

He shrugged. 'I dunno, it's Mel's I think.' Griff attempted a casual grin, playing it cool, but seeing my disdain it morphed into a lewd smirk.

'But these might be her panties,' he sneered.

He opened the buttons of his flies to reveal he was wearing a pair of lacy women's knickers. I didn't know where to look or what to say. I felt the colour rising in my cheeks, my fingers tensing into fists.

'What's wrong Ga, are you jealous?'

'Fuck off!' I shouted and lunged towards him. It wasn't my style to swear and lose my cool, but I wasn't in control any more.

Griff held his palms up to calm me. And then he said something that stopped me in my tracks. He spoke the words that have haunted me ever since:

'I didn't sleep with Bethan, okay, or any of her friends, and I never have and I never will. Are you really so blind? Don't you understand, it's her brother that I want?'

And with that, he kissed me. Griff kissed me full on the lips.

For a second or two, I hesitated. Then I hit him. Hit him as hard as I could and watched him crumble pitifully to the ground at my feet. I stood over him panting and screaming:

'Fuck off, puff! You're sick, you are. You're ill, seriously ill!'

And with that I turned and ran away, confused and shaking, leaving him sprawled on the ground with blood on his lips, his mascara smudged and his flies still open. When I got home, I drank two glasses of water and retched into the sink, trying to cleanse the taste of his lips from my mouth.

I never spoke with Griff again. We went our separate ways. Kept apart. A few months later, a week after his eighteenth birthday, he was dead. God knows what was going through his mind that day. High on poppers and vodka, mixed up, fucked up, this is where he came to die. To escape. To jump headlong from life when he could no longer see any *brighter sides*. Where we'd always come. And before he died he scraped his own epitaph into the rock. It simply said, *Still ill*.

The clouds have closed in now and a squally rain is arrowing in from the west. No one else will come now. I clear the moss from around the crudely engraved words and run my fingers along the indentations, tracing the shapes of the letters. Soon, the elements will erase them forever.

I lay the flowers I'd brought in my knapsack in the shelter of the outcrop, then turn to leave. There's no point lingering any longer. No point dredging up old memories. Reproaching myself for things I did and said when I was seventeen. What good can come from regurgitating the taste of his lips once again. Or recalling how, on that day in May all those years ago, I'd almost kissed him back.

Dog Days

'Is there someone up there?'

Siwan puts her binoculars down and reaches for the knife strapped against her thigh, her heart beating faster. Through the branches, she can just make out the face of a little boy peering up into the tree. She relaxes her grip on the handle of the knife, he's only small. He'll go away soon enough if she keeps still.

'I can see you,' says the boy. 'I know you're up there.'

Siwan sighs. She could do without this now. This is her den.

'Shwsh, be quiet you fool. Now, go away!'

Silence. Hopefully, he's heeded her advice and moved on.

'Can I come up?'

He's bold, this one, and stupid too. Or desperate.

'No, I said go away and leave me alone.'

'I'm good at climbing trees.'

'Well go and find your own tree then.' She considers swearing at him, but he doesn't deserve that.

Silence again. She parts the leaves to look down. The boy has gone. She heaves a sigh of relief and lays back against the trunk in her nook. How did he manage to see her up here? She thought she was well hidden. She will need to be more careful.

From her position high in the canopy, Siwan can survey the slope down to the dual carriageway. The bark is rough and knobbly and crawling with annoying ants, but she is used to it now. She has gazed out from this vantage point so many times that she knows every miniscule detail of the scene below. All that traffic heading north. Where is it all going? Not that anything is moving now. It's gridlock.

Siwan likes to make up stories about the vehicles and their occupants. It whiles away the time.

There's the family in the red SUV heading off for their caravan on the coast, the children singing, or playing I spy, or scrolling through their messages on their phones as their parents fret in the unmoving queue. The man in the black BMW that stinks of putrid aftershave and new leather. He has run away from his family, left them behind in the mire of the city. Droplets of perspiration scurry down his brow as he rams his fist against the horn and curses loudly. Then there's the woman wearing a boiler suit in the dirty white van. She is listening to a podcast of conversational French, lost in her own thoughts, unaware of the chaos in the world around her. *Je suis tres heureuse*, she repeats to herself, staring out into the fumes billowing from the exhausts. In the articulated lorry, the driver is thinking of the girl he'd seen in the service station earlier, the one with the red hair and freckles that smiled at him shyly. He's going to find her. There's something he needs to say to her before it's too late.

Only one car is heading in the opposite direction, towards the city. This has a young woman in it. Siwan thinks she is probably racing to see her mother or her husband, or maybe her child. All that frustration and futile rage on the other side of the central reservation, but for her, the road is clear. She is gripping the steering wheel tightly, foot hard on the accelerator. But she'll be coughing and wheezing as she's driving, her eyesight blurred with tears.

Siwan leans back and closes her eyes as the dappled rays of the afternoon caress her skin. She shouldn't let her imagination run away with her. It will give her nightmares. She listens to the tits chirruping in the branches above her. She's safe. Everything will be alright.

She is drifting off to sleep when something small and hard whacks against her calf. She opens her eyes and rubs her leg. Perhaps a squirrel dropped a nut from above? But then another missile pings against her arm. It's a conker, and it's come from her side somewhere. It couldn't have come from a squirrel, unless they had learnt to hurl things horizontally. She turns and looks in the direction from where the nut came. The boy is perched on the branch of a nearby tree, grinning back at her. He has a handful of ammo in his palms. He flings another conker in her direction.

'Told you I was good at climbing trees,' he says.

Siwan glares at him. 'I thought I told you to go away.'

'You told me to find my own tree, so I did,' he says. He's clambered quite high up, but his perch is easily visible and there are no secure places for sitting or sleeping like in her tree. He won't be able to stay there for long. She decides the best thing is to ignore him. If he's still there by sunset, she'll chase him off.

'Do you have any food?' he says.

'No.'

'So what's in those bags?'

Siwan tightens her grip on her two knapsacks. 'Nothing.'

'Only, I'm really hungry.'

'I told you, I haven't got any food.'

The boy stops talking, but she can hear him humming something to himself. It's a familiar tune about a postman and a cat. He should be quiet. She clenches her fists and clamps them against her ears. Crack. A conker strikes her brow just above her eye. It's still in its spiky casing. *The cheeky sod!* She grabs her knife and points it towards the boy in the adjacent tree.

'You do that again and I'll come over there and cut your little boy's bits off and shove them down your throat, do you hear?' she growls.

'You're Siwan Morris, aren't you?' says the boy cheerfully, unperturbed by the threat.

Siwan scowls back at the boy. How does he know her name?

'You were in my sister's class at school. Her name's Gwennan. Gwennan Edwards. You came over for a sleepover on her fifteenth birthday last year. You had pizza and watched vampire films and then you slept out in a tent on the back lawn. Mam said you'd sneaked a bottle of vodka out during the night and when she went out in the morning someone had been sick all over her statue of the Buddha.'

Siwan smiles briefly at the recollection. 'It was tequila, not vodka,' she says.

And it was her, Siwan, who'd thrown up – a stinking syrup of cheese, pepperoni, crisps and chocolate birthday cake in a coca-cola and tequila sauce. The Buddha had seemed to be cupping his hands, as if he was attempting to catch the vomit. They'd had a right laugh that night telling ghost stories, pretending to be vampires and swigging from the tequila – but her head hurt like hell the next day. When was that? It must only have been last year, but it feels like a lifetime ago now.

So he must be Gwennan's younger brother. He was annoying back then too, as she recalls, trying to sneak in and watch the films with them, dancing around the tents and tripping over the guy-lines when he should have been in bed. But he was kind of cute too. She doesn't want to ask, but she can't help herself.

'Is Gwennan... are you with...?' The words get stuck.

The boy looks sad and shakes his head. 'She's, you know, like mum and dad... and the others.'

Siwan had suspected this much. Gwennan was six months older, after all.

'Are you sure you haven't got any food?' says the boy.

She studies him more closely now. His clothes are torn and his face is dirty and scarred. He is emaciated, his skin stretched taut over his cheekbones, eyes bulging in their sockets. Under his arm he's clutching a tattered teddy-bear. She looks away. She cannot feel anything. She has to keep her heart hard and her mind clear.

'If I give you something, will you go away?'

'I suppose.' The boy sounds disappointed.

'Promise?'

'I promise.'

'Because if you don't, I swear I'll come over and do what I said I'd do with this knife, even if you are Gwennan's brother.'

She reaches in to her bag and pulls out a full packet of quavers, her favourite. She reconsiders and rummages through her bag again. She finds the half-eaten packet of cheese and onion crisps from earlier. She checks it's knotted securely and tosses the packet out of the tree to the floor. 'Here you go,' she says.

She watches him scurry down the tree towards the packet and crouch to pick it up and open it. He clasps the bag and scoffs the remaining contents like a skittish rodent, his eyes darting around nervously.

After he finishes the last crumbs of the crisps, he tears the bag open and licks at the insides before discarding the remains of the packet. He looks up at Siwan, his eyes wide and expectant.

'Now go,' she hisses.

'Thank you,' he says, rubbing at the corner of his eyes with his bony little fingers. He turns and slumps off through the trees, kicking at the leaf litter as he goes. *Take care*, she mouths silently to herself, but she is relieved to be alone again.

Siwan wonders where he will go. It was nice having another human to talk to, she supposes. And it would be quite nice if he could have stayed so that she could look after him, but she realises that is not feasible. She understands the laws of the jungle.

Now he has gone, she resumes her surveillance of the valley below. In the distance a large black cloud of smoke is rising into the sky and she notices that there is a faint acrid tang in the air, like burning rubber. There must be a fire somewhere. She takes out her binoculars and scans the vicinity, but she can't see anything to indicate the cause. She idly wonders if it was started accidentally or deliberately.

Siwan is about to put her binoculars away when she catches some movement on the road. She adjusts the lens. Someone is there among the traffic. She zooms in. A figure is crossing the north-bound carriageway. It's the little boy, Gwennan's brother. He still has the teddy in his hand. Doesn't he know how dangerous the road is? He's ambling between the column of vehicles - the red SUV, the black BMW, the dirty white van, the articulated lorry. He isn't taking much care, stopping to look in through each window, trying at the doors.

He won't find anything. Siwan's already looked.

She watches as the boy straddles the central reservation and ambles up to the single hatchback which has come to rest against the kerb of the hard shoulder on the way in towards the city. He is exposed here, in the open. The boy walks around to the passenger side and tries the door. It opens. She can see him lean over and crawl inside. She wonders what he'll find. What state the woman is in by now? Will her stinking corpse still be sitting there, or is she no more than a skeleton, slumped against the steering wheel?

Siwan scans the road. Something else is moving among the stationary cars on the northbound side. Figures skulking noiselessly on four legs between the vehicles. She zooms in on the largest of the dogs until she can see the drooling tongue lolling in its mouth, the great yellow fangs, the cruel, dead eyes.

The boy has clambered back out of the car. He's holding something in his hands. It looks as if he's found a stash of boiled sweets in the glove compartment. She must have missed these. He is trying to peel the sticky wrapping off one of the sweets. He looks happy. Behind him the shadows creep across the tarmac, surrounding the vehicle.

Siwan removes the binoculars. She doesn't wait to see what comes next.

She knows she has to act now, while there's still time. She gathers her stuff together and shinnies down the tree. The dogs will be diverted, it's her chance to get away. Silently, she scuttles off into the trees in the opposite direction.

In a Flash

Gavin traces the igam-ogam of the frail blue line with a matchstick until it rests upon a little beige coloured rectangle cwtched between the winding river and the straight black railway track. The rectangle with *Sch* written next to it. His lips curl into a smile. It's a smile, but it looks like a sneer.

At school, Gavin was good at reading maps. It was the only thing he was good at. He remembers a geography lesson with Miss Jenkins out in the demountable: 'Miss, the school is in grid square 4473'.

Her saying, 'Well done, Gavin, you clever little boy.' Her blazing red lips. The glow he felt inside.

Only Miss Jenkins had ever called him clever.

Now, under his touch, the contours spring out of the paper like a 3D model, as if the map were written in braille. He can see and feel the hills and hollows of the topography as clearly as if he were stroking his fingers over Miss Jenkins' soft, naked body.

Gavin stabs the match on the summit of the hill above the school. This is where he came to get away from the cruel teachers, the dull teachers, the couldn't-give-a-shit-if-he-lived-or-died teachers. All the teachers that weren't Miss Jenkins. On the map, the slopes are shaded green. But Gavin knows things the map doesn't know. He knows they should be black now, not green.

Because today it looks different. Today it's just a knotty stubble of charred tree trunks scattered over the valley sides like soot-black gravestones. He remembers the raging fires, the intense heat enveloping him, the thick black fumes flooding his lungs. Afterwards, the damp black bark crumbled in his hands, staining his fingers. He'd muzzled his face in his palms and gulped in the intoxicating aroma of fresh, burnt wood until the carbon coursed through his veins.

Gavin strikes the match and studies it, transfixed, inhaling deeply. The flame shimmers like an amber tulip, cupped in translucent blue petals. It dies away in a puff of curled smoke. The withered stub is a shrunken head on a stick.

He tosses the match away and strikes another. When he blows, the flame flickers and gyrates. It dances for him. It does as he bids. 'Go, my sweet,' he says, 'go burn!'

A dark shadow creeps across the map as the paper stains and shrivels. He watches as the landscape ignites, as the flames engulf the fields and the farms, the A roads and B roads and bridleways, the radio masts and triangulation pillars, the churches with spires and churches with towers, the public houses and public conveniences. Destroying every little beige building along the valley floor until only brittle flakes and ashes remain.

Square 4473 is swallowed up in the inferno. Everything extinguished in a flash. Everything except for a few girders and slates, and the geography classroom on the far side of the yard where they used to line up for the fire drills.

Gavin smiles. Or maybe he sneers. He's a clever boy.

Fault Lines

It's nineteen minutes past two.

Faint rays of sunlight caress the hard, dead ground. New life sprouts from the darkness. Birds serenade you with their spring songs. You feel something stir deep inside. Is it hope or faith that makes you change your plans? That makes you believe the doctors might be wrong. That it's worth trying one more time.

You worry, as you drive into the estate, that perhaps you should have bought fresh flowers. Then you look down at the daffodil on your lapel and you think, that will do, even if it's not a real one. After all, you have something silk and skimpy in the bag, much more to his taste. And you have the wine, the bottle of Montalcino to celebrate Saint David, and to remember Saint Valentine and the weekend in Rome, just two weeks ago.

Maybe you've both been trying too hard. Love should be impulsive. Isn't that what he is always saying? That it has become too mechanical. That the thrill has gone. When he comes home, he will be surprised to see you. In a negligee with a glass of wine in hand. He will be aroused. It will be like it was before, like it was in Rome in the hotel. It was just the wrong time then, that's all. But now is right, you know it's right. You've got the charts. You can feel it.

This is what is on your mind as you park outside your house in the little close where you live. All your senses are turned inwards on the vibrations and rhythms of your own body so that you do not see or hear the warning signs. You recognise his car parked in the drive in the afternoon when he should be at work, but you do not notice the eerie silence, the sudden absence of birdsong. You don't see the other car outside. The familiar car straddling the kerb like a great gaping fissure, slashing the tarmac in two. When you step over the crevice and into the house and hear the music upstairs, you don't feel the earth shift under your feet, or see the walls ripple and buckle. You don't see or hear any of these things because you are kind and generous and trust in people. Trust in your husband. You only think that he must not be feeling well, that he must have come home early and gone to bed because he's ill.

So when you walk into the bedroom and see the devastation before you, you cannot comprehend what it is you are looking at: the clothes scattered across the floor, the duvet crumpled and creased, the figures writhing as if in pain, the panic and shock and fear. A glass topples in slow motion from the bedside-table and shatters on the tiled floor. The wine seeps from it, like blood from an open wound.

For a moment, time snags like a record caught in a groove. The scene is a snapshot of captured motion. Everything is blurred. It makes no sense. He is lying there naked and still, a look of horror frozen on his face. He reminds you of one of those Roman statues. His mouth is open, but no words come out.

Then time jerks forward again and you sense movement. Another figure is stumbling from the wreckage of the bed. She sits on the far edge, dishevelled and confused, holding her head in her hands. The woman turns and looks up at you. Looks up at you with desperate pleading eyes, and you see that it is Sara. She is mumbling something. She is saying, 'I'm sorry, Helen, I'm so sorry, we didn't think... please forgive me.' The CD player starts to play your song. He switches it off before the lyrics begin. Everything goes quiet.

All is tranquil now except for the steady nagging tick-tock of your alarm clock and a distant rumbling that you can't quite place. Somewhere deep in your core a pulse becomes a throb, becomes a thump, pounding behind the bridge of your nose. Hot, viscous lava bubbles through your veins. Your eyes stream and burn. The noise gets louder and louder until it is screeching in your head like nails on a blackboard. Then the waves hit you. A tsunami of nausea surging through your body and crystallising into a single guttural word. Even then it's held back. Not fully let go. The hard *eff* followed by an almost whispered *uck*, suspended in the air like a prayer to some primeval god. A god called Fuck for a fucked up world. Then it comes again, wave after wave after wave, 'Fuck! Fuck! Fuck!' screamed into the room like an incantation. You do not see the irony in this.

It is so unlike you. You hardly ever swear. Only rarely, when you'd drunk too much. We used to call it your tobacco tongue – you'd drink and then you'd smoke and then you'd swear and then you'd giggle yourself into a deep intoxicated slumber. Perhaps one day you will sit again with your girlfriends in a bar in Mill Lane and recount through whoops of laughter, '... *and you'll never believe what I said when I found them at it?*'

Except that Sara is one of those girlfriends. She's your best friend. The one who knows your secrets and dreams and who would understand. The only one who you could ever say that to.

And you're sober now. You've never been more sober. It feels as if you've slumbered in an alcoholic stupor for fourteen years and awoken to find that all that went before was just a drunken sham.

'Get out!' you implore. 'Get the fuck out of my house!'

In that moment your husband seems unsure if you're talking just to Sara, or to the both of them. Whether you want him to collect up his clothes too and leave the house. To leave his own house. He does not yet perceive that this is the moment that his house will become your house. The moment that your life together will become two separate lives. Your life and his life. Two continents ripped apart across a fault line.

Sara grabs her clothes and skulks for the door. On her way she places her hand on your arm and says,

'I'm truly, truly sorry,' but your hands are over your ears and you don't hear Sara's words, you only see the bitch who has deflowered the sanctity of your home, your bed, your marriage.

As she leaves, Sara glances briefly at your husband. Her face is crumpled with shock and pain. She hesitates for a moment and then she is gone. She has pulled herself free.

It is just you and him now. Even though you have seen him naked a thousand times before, you realise you are truly seeing him undressed for the first time. Seeing him without the cosmetics of his little fictions and lies, right through to the naked core of his desires and deceits below. You see the guile, the pretence, the fraud. You remember the vows and valentine cards and all the tests and failures and tears. How, when you threw those coins into the Roman fountain to wish for the gift of a child, it wasn't what he was wishing for at all. When he closed his eyes, he was probably thinking only of kissing Sara, wishing only to cavort with her again between the sheets. Between your sheets.

Silver coins and kisses.

You try to process what you've seen. You are caught in the ash cloud, helpless in the pyroclastic flow as it sweeps over you and your life, vaporising all that was past. You stand petrified like the figures in Pompeii. The light has gone out in your eyes. Your heart has been turned to stone.

And you see now that nothing lasts forever. The eternal city didn't last forever. For you, it didn't even last three weeks. When the earth moves, when the volcano blows, there is no warning. No reason. It happens, and then everything that was there before comes tumbling down; buildings and statues and gods.

So as you look at him now, you see only a man. A weak man squirming before you, clenching his fist into a ball to hide his greatest shame, to hide the little plastic sack of life, of love, of the ultimate betrayal. The little sack of babies you crave so much. Dreams that will be so casually washed away.

'Go,' you whisper, 'just go.'

You wait in silence as he dresses. You ask no questions and he gives you no answers. He knows that it's futile. You can see now that everything he's ever said was empty, like all the words he writes. His little stories. Those little lies he weaves. Even now he's writing these lines. Your lines. Infusing your character with thoughts and emotions. Thoughts only you know, things only you can feel and nobody else.

You watch as he slinks out of the bedroom. Watch as he creeps past the nursery; the shrine to the one that never was. The one that never came. The one that might have changed everything.

As he puts on his shoes and his coat you take down the card from the fireplace. It says, *To my darling wife on Valentine's day.* You re-read the words and count the crosses. Then you shred the card into tiny pieces and take the single red rose from the vase. Its withered petals crumble like paper in your fist.

Your eyes follow him as he staggers out of the door and slumps into his car; as he steps across the fault line and out of your life for good. He winds the window down and opens his mouth to speak, but he can find no words. The Earth has moved, there is nothing to be said. So you stand in the ruins of your marriage and watch him drive away. Watch him fade into the distance, getting smaller and smaller until he is no more.

You walk out into the middle of the street in a daze.

Faint rays of sunlight caress the hard, dead ground. New life sprouts from the darkness. Birds serenade you with their spring songs.

It's nineteen minutes to three.

Words are like Birds

Once upon a time, Michael was happy. It was a longlongtimeago.

Michael sits glumly in his living room brooding over the news that Llinos has just given him. He shuts his eyes and spins his chair roundandround until his head is giddy and empty. It feels like he's flying. When he stops and opens his eyes, his thoughts continue to churn and bobble like a bottle on a stormy ocean.

Llinos is in the kitchen, singing to herself in Welsh. An orchestra of clanking pots and slamming doors and splashing water accompanies her. He leans back and listens as his dizziness subsides. He likes listening to her singing or talking in her native tongue. A waterfall of words cascading over him. Mysterious sounds and meanings in a language with mutations. Michael loves the idea that words should mutate and metamorphose into something else. He imagines words emerging like butterflies from a cocoon and flying away from the cage of their previous meaning. Words flying free like birds.

Wirds like birds and bords like words.

By the time Llinos enters with the flowers, Michael is hunched over his desk, scrawling something onto paper. The pencil quakes like a seismograph in his hand as he draws.

She arranges an assortment of vases around the room and opens the curtains and windows. She flits from one to the other. She is a fairy dispelling light and colour.

'That's better,' she says brightly. 'A little bit of sunshine and freshness.'

Michael wrinkles his nose at the sickly scent of the flowers and glowers. 'So you're finally flying the nest?' he says.

'Yes, I am. I'm flying away. Tweet, tweet, tweet, tweet! I'm going to college to learn how to become a great artist.' Llinos opens a small brown bottle and pours a thick amber liquid onto a plastic spoon.

'When did you say you are going?'

'Sunday.'

Michael frowns.

'Don't worry, I'll be back at holidays to see you.'

'If I'm still here.'

'Don't be silly, Michael. Where would you go?'

The frown becomes a scowl. 'You'll forget about me'.

'No, I won't. Soon as I get back, I'll come and visit. I promise. And anyway, I'll see you again tomorrow. We're going to the seaside, remember? Now then, open wide.'

Llinos hovers above him and spoons the treacly liquid through his pursed lips. She smells of chlorine and honeyed lemons.

'So what are you doing there, Mikey?' she says, peeking down at the piece of paper on Michael's lap.

'I'm drawing something.'

'Well I can see that, buddy, but what are you drawing?'

'As you're going to art school, I thought I'd draw you a picture. A souvenir to remind you of me.'

'That's kind of you. What is it?'

'Can't you tell?'

Llinos squints and studies the lines and hieroglyphics on the page, searching for something recognisable. 'Is it an angel?'

'It's a picture of you,' he says. 'It's called, *Deep in the dark depths of December the demure dreaming damsel dances divinely.*'

'Oh.'

'My artistically illiterate illustration is a literate translation of the alliteration,' he explains.

Llinos doesn't understand. She doesn't expect to understand. They'd grown up together and he was always coming out with things like this. Multitudes of jumbled words that swoop and dive in strange patterns like a murmuration of starlings. She lets them fly and dance over her.

'Well it's nice, Michael, but it's not that flattering, is it?' She holds the picture next to her face for him to compare the two. 'And why have you drawn wings on me?'

'It's abstract art, Llinos. Subversion through squiggles. My pencil is my Kalashnikov. Actually, I'm drawing you as a butterfly,' he says, 'like the one in the story.'

'What story's that, Mikey?' She quickly inserts a second spoonful into his mouth before he can turn his head away. Michael scrunches up his face and gulps it down.

'You know, the one about the tadpole and the caterpillar who fall in love. It's a sort of fairy story. I borrowed it from the hospital.'

'I don't know that story, Mikey.'

'It's meant for children, but it's quite gory. There's a tadpole that lives in a pond and he falls in love with this caterpillar in the tree above. He calls her his beautiful rainbow, and she calls him her shiny black pearl. They love each other very much, but they come from different worlds. She lives in the sky with the trees and the flowers and he lives in a deep, dark pond. They hope one day they will be able to be together, but of course, they can't change their circumstances.'

'So what happens?'

'She turns into a butterfly and flies away. Just like you. You are my beautiful rainbow, Llinos, and you're turning into a butterfly and flying away.'

'Oh, and you're my shiny black pearl, Michael.'

'Yes, but I've turned into an ugly frog and I'll never be able to fly like you.'

Michael's face is so serious and glum that Llinos can't resist smiling.

'Don't say that, Mikey, you're not a frog, you're more of a toad, really,' she says, her eyes twinkling. 'So, does the story have a happy ending? Don't tell me. She comes back and kisses the frog and he turns into a handsome prince and they fly away together and live happily ever after?' Before he can answer she leans over and kisses him on the forehead, then stands back, rubbing her chin mock-seriously to consider his face.

'Let me see,' she says, 'no, that doesn't seem to have worked.'

'Haha, very funny,' he says, 'actually, that's not what happens.'

'Are you trying to say something, Michael? Because all I can hear is *ribbit, ribbit, ribbit.*'

'I'm glad you find me so amusing,' he says. 'Have you quite finished?'

'I'm sorry,' she says, biting her lip, 'I'm only pulling your leg... it's just that you've got such long froggy legs, they're so easy to pull.' Llinos whoops and jigs, her face sparkling with mirth.

Michael squats miserably in his chair until he can take no more. 'Oh,... eff off, will you!' he bellows at her, but Llinos is on a roll:

'Don't you mean hop off, not eff off?' Llinos bursts into gleeful laughter, hopping and flapping her arms until Michael's grimace thaws into a smile and he starts chuckling too.

'You know, I wish I really could fly like a butterfly,' she says.

'Huh, I'd just like to walk again, never mind fly,' he says. They both glance down at the useless stump of his body.

'Oh Michael, cariad bach,' she sighs, 'you know you'll always be a prince to me.' Llinos leans over and enfolds him in a big hug, burying him in her bosom so that Michael finds himself staring straight into the deep dark chasm of her cleavage. An amber slug of saliva slithers onto his tongue and oozes from the corner of his mouth. It dribbles down his chin, leaving a slimy sugary trail in its wake and a sticky damp smudge of mucus, like a broach, upon her breast.

Before she leaves, Llinos deposits a packet of tablets and a small jar of pills on the desk in front of Michael and reminds him to put sun-tan lotion on before she picks him up tomorrow.

'And be nice to Clair this afternoon,' she says. 'Clair tells me you're not taking your medication when you should.'

'Yes I am,' he lies.

'They'll take the pain away, Michael. You should take them.'

'They're trying to poison me, Llinos. Poison my mind with happiness. I don't want to be happy. I just want to be me.'

'It's good to be happy, Michael.' Llinos examines his anguished expression and a shadow passes momentarily across her face. She smiles vacantly. 'Well, I suppose it's time for me to eff off now, Michael.' With that, she disappears through the door, leaving the drawing behind on his desk.

Llinos doesn't like it, he concludes. He scrunches the paper up into a grenade and tosses it onto the floor.

Michael is pensive after Llinos has gone, incubating the news she has left behind and reflecting darkly on the implications. He doesn't want to be sedated or placated. He doesn't want their drugs invading his mind or colonising his thoughts or anaesthetising his emotions. Turning him into some unthinking and unfeeling vegetable. He doesn't want to think like they want him to think or to feel like they want him to feel. It's intellectual castration. It's the one part of him that works. The one bit that's free.

His words are like birds but his words and deeds are not feathered friends; his ducks are not all lined up; his swallows never make summers; he has many in the hand but never any in the bush. Michael is the ugly duckling who turns into an ugly duck. He feels trapped like a canary in a cage.

When Clair arrives, Michael is fizzing with agitation. As usual she is professional and distant and full of patronising platitudes. Her language is as factual and functional as bricks. Rules and regulations. Do's and don'ts. Making letters into fetters. Walls of words incarcerating him, suffocating him, pushing him under.

He grunts and nods compliantly as she speaks. He calls it conversational minimalism. Stone-age retro. There is no point wasting words on her. She wouldn't understand. They go over her head.

Clair shows him pamphlets and diagrams. She talks in cold sensible syntax about strategies for coping and about formulating support plans. She uses words like 'managing' and 'palliative', not words like 'hope' or 'cure'.

For Clair, language is no more than a bodily function. Speaking is like excreting. Words are like turds.

They sit there steaming, long after she's gone.

That night, Michael dreams he can fly. He dreams he has angel-wings and that he's free to fly to the end of the rainbow. He soars high above the landscape like Icarus, towards a glittering golden sun. The sun has Llinos's face. Her arms are outstretched, but he cannot reach her. The further he flies, the further she recedes into the distance. 'Llinos, Llinos!' he cries. 'Don't leave me. Please don't go!' Hallucinations haunt him like wasps at a picnic table. He wriggles and writhes on his bed, thrashing at the buzzing visions. The sun is laughing at him. Llinos is laughing and waving goodbye. She's saying, 'eff off Michael, it's time to eff off!'

The sea is calm the next day. Michael listens to the gentle rhythm of the waves below and the lullabies of the gulls above. It feels like home. He wonders what it would be like to swim once more in a salty sea. He wonders, but he knows it will never happen. It's one of many hundreds of sensations he'll never have again. His world is shrinking. The quality and quantity of his experiences are diminishing day by day. He's a train trundling towards a tunnel or a broken bridge. Except, it's more of a shuffling. A festination to his destination.

And Llinos is leaving. His beautiful rainbow is leaving. He watches her silhouetted against the evening sun, her hair fluttering in the breeze. She seems exotic and strange to him now. She's changed. Llinos is no longer the girl he knew. She is all womanly curves and grace.

If only she would stay. But he knows there are no fairy stories. There are no happy endings. Princesses don't really kiss frogs. And would he want her to be a part of his world? To hear the voices in his head? To see the stinking swamp of his existence, the dark, perverted sewers of his mind? The lust and bile and bitterness?

Llinos turns towards him. She is wearing the sun like a halo.

'You seem so sad, Michael,' she says. 'What's wrong?'

'I don't want you to go, Llinos. I'll miss you.'

'I'll miss you too, Michael. But I must go. You know I must go.'

Against his will, Michael begins to cry. Before he knows it, he is sobbing uncontrollably. Llinos perches on the edge of his wheelchair. She takes his hand and strokes his hair.

'Llinos,' he croaks, 'without you, I no longer want to...'

'Shwsh now Michael, I understand. I know what it is you want. Take these, they will help you.'

She pops a couple of pills on his tongue. He pulls them into his mouth and swallows them like flies. Flies made of butter.

'Shall we go and see the sunset now, before it's too late?' she says.

Llinos pushes Michael's wheelchair up to the cliff's edge and lifts him gently up so that he is able to peer down at the swirling abyss below. He stands trembling in the wind, a fragile bundle of fasciculation in her tight embrace. He has the sense that he is suspended somewhere between the land and the sea. That he is no longer a part of the continent.

'This is it,' she says.

A bridge of shimmering golden sunlight stretches out across the ocean to the horizon; to the very edge of the world. It seems so close he could almost touch it. A little hop and he'd be there. All around him, gulls are soaring and cackling. His head begins to throb and spin, and the sun seems to swell and pulsate before his eyes. He feels sure that it's calling him. It's telling him to eff off.

Michael laughs. The idea amuses him. The thought of escaping a language where even phonetics isn't spelt fonetically. Words are like birds, they should be free. He decides there will be no more phucking ephs. He'll eph oph!

He looks out one last time. The gulls have phlown into the dusk. They have phorgotten him. They will all phorget him.

'It's time,' she says. 'Time to go.'

Michael opens his arms to the wind. Llinos relaxes her grip so that only her phairy phingers like pheathers hold him phrom phalling.

'See Michael, you're not a phrog,' she says. 'You can stand by yourselph. And if you phlap your wings, I bet you could phly and be as phree as the birds. It's a leap of phaith, Michael, that's all.'

So Michael closes his eyes and phlaps and phlaps until he can pheel himselph phloating, then he phlys away to a place no one will ever phind.

Somewhere pharpharaway.

Acknowledgements

The stories in this collection have been written over a ten-year period and some have previously been published in other publications or have received recognition in competitions:

The Birthday Gift was the winner of the Hilda Mckenzie trophy – the Cardiff Writers' Circle short story competition, 2018.
Waiting for Lift-off was runner-up in the same competition in 2020.
Moonhorses won the Yellow Room short story competition, 2012.
Smoke gets in your Eyes was runner-up in Word Hut 1000 word short story competition, March 2013.
Stil ill was runner-up in the Allen Raine short story competition, 2011
The Last Knight was the winner of the Cardiff Writers' Circle flash-fiction competition, 2020.
In a Flash was long-listed for the Multi-story flash fiction competition in 2012 & short-listed for the Flash 500 competition, December 2012.

Diolch/Thanks:

I'd like to thank the following for their support, help and/or inspiration:

My fellow writers: Alex Falconer, Claude Annik Rapport and Martin Rhys, have been constant writing companions and provided oodles of useful advice and feedback in relation to many of the stories in this collection.

The members of Cardiff Writers' Circle under the chairmanship of Paul Jauregui. The Zoom meetings during the Covid lockdown were really appreciated.

Various musiciens, bands and songwriters whose songs were the original inspiration for so many stories and ideas.

Rhys Davies – the most talented Welsh artist in the USA, for his wonderful work on the covers and his friendship. Diolch yn fawr iawn.

Diolch hefyd i Eirian - xxx

And finally, the usual hello to Jason Isaacs.

About the Author

Eryl Samuel lives near Cardiff with his family and assistant editor (the cat). His first novel, **Cat's Eyes**, was published in 2020. **Words are Like Birds** is his first published volume of short stories.